FALLEN STARS

FALLEN STARS

STEVE BROWN

Chick Springs Publishing
Taylors, SC

10   9   8   7   6   5   4   3   2   1

For Bernard Fall

ACKNOWLEDGMENTS

My thanks to the reading group:
Missy Johnson, Ellen Smith, Susannah Farley,
Dwight Watt, Richard Goebel, Mark Brown, Kate Lehman,
Bill Jenkins, and fellow Wolfhound, Fred Kramer,
and, of course, Mary Ella.

"Following my wife's departure from Vietnam, she was driving in Honolulu when she heard over her car radio that I had been assassinated."

A Soldier Reports
by General William Westmoreland

CHAPTER
ONE

Long Bien, South Vietnam

S he was going out today. After all the stalling and bullshit the army could muster, she was finally being taken on one of the commanding general's flyovers. All you had to do was stay on the army's butt and anything was possible. Casey Blackburn leaned against the metal building, warm to her back, smoked a hasty cigarette, and tried to ignore the midday heat, humidity, and derisive remarks from the helicopter crews. The soldiers smoked and joked inside the hangar, so Casey stood outside.

She'd seen them openly staring at her. It was more than being the only white woman they'd seen in months, it was the attitude she ran into everywhere. Not that garbage about taking a job away from a man, but what the hell was she doing here? Was she crazy? Most of the GIs didn't want to be here and would give their left nut to be back home in the "Real World," as the grunts called the States. It was simple, as she'd explained more than once. For a reporter Vietnam was where the action was, so here she was.

Dropping her cigarette to the ground and snubbing it out with her government-issue boot, Casey considered how lucky she was to even be here. A few months ago she'd been just another reporter covering the Chicago police blotter, with only dreams of reporting from 'Nam. Then Lady Luck interceded. And luck had to be a woman because the suspect the police held in custody would talk only to Casey, had picked her and her blond hair out of the crowd of clamoring reporters.

This psycho had dismembered seven young women and stashed most of their body parts in freezers in his basement, and Casey'd had the exclusive. She'd also had the shakes and an empty stomach from having tossed her cookies at the conclusion of every interview. That's how graphic the descriptions of his killings had been. He was a stalker, finding, following, and luring young women into his lair. It was the mid-sixties. The rules were changing, so the monster had plenty of victims to choose from. Girls from abusive families saw kids on TV demonstrating against the war and realized they didn't have to take this crap anymore. They could run away. And some did—right into the arms, into the freezer of this psychopath.

Yes, she'd seen the evidence. It'd been a condition of the exclusive. But Casey was determined to keep her cool and never let on that before viewing the evidence, she hadn't eaten all day—and she'd still thrown up! Twice. The dry heaves were the worst. Her body had been flat out of control. And the longer she talked to this nut, the more she became convinced that he thought he'd beat the rap and *she'd* be his next victim, ending up in pieces in a freezer in some basement. The fact that the psycho's collection of heads had been exclusively made up of blondes hadn't been lost on Casey.

The wacko hadn't beaten the rap, and the only remorse he'd shown was regret at not being able to continue seeing her. At their last meeting he'd stared at her long blond hair, as if taking a mental snapshot for his long incarceration. Hell, maybe the jerk thought he'd break out and track her down. Well, good luck, buster; she was off to Vietnam—but that didn't come right away. No, that took a bit of time and a lot more doing.

Rumor had it that the president would ask Congress for upwards of half a million men. Casey's mentor, an older man and professor, told her this nut case had given her credentials, that she should apply for one of the many openings in the expanding news bureaus in Saigon. Don't miss this war, he advised her. It'll be the only war of your generation.

So Casey interviewed several editors, talked rather grandiosely about being raised as an army brat, and how she knew her way around the military after living overseas . . . and failed to get one of those many jobs.

Marguerite Higgins had just died from some rare tropical disease while reporting from South Vietnam. It seemed every editor had heard how Marguerite wasted away, how the dying reporter called her children into her hospital room and kissed them good-bye. No editor wanted a death like that on his conscience.

But, Casey argued, she didn't have children and wasn't married. Besides, Marguerite had been given her chance to report from more than one war. Why not Casey Blackburn?

No way, the editors said. They would save this fool from herself.

Undismayed, Casey took things in her own hands and flew to the Far East, then sneaked into Hanoi and returned with "What Uncle Ho Wants." But it wasn't what the State Department wanted, and they let her publisher know about it. The day she was fired, Casey sold the story to a wire service and found an editor who liked women "with balls." Two weeks later, Casey left Chicago with more luggage than she'd need and sore arms from too many inoculations—she'd made damn sure of that! After suffering through a flight of over twenty-four hours, she had arrived in the war zone. But until today, she hadn't been allowed to go out with the CIC—commander in charge.

On the other side of the landing strip, the door to the flight center opened. The general, radio call sign "Falcon One," walked out, an aide and another reporter behind him. To the general's left and down the flight line roosted the fat-bodied Hueys like the one they'd be going up in. Beside them sat the narrow-faced gunships that would fly shotgun and one or two Chinooks not necessary for a mission like this. "Shit-hooks," as the grunts had nicknamed them, were huge, oversized helicopters able to lift jeeps, trucks, or whole platoons of men out of the jungle.

As Falcon crossed the landing strip, Casey could see

the general was not pleased. Ever since arriving in-country Casey had become one of the reporters asking all the wrong questions at the Five O'clock Follies, the name reporters had given the army's daily press briefings.

Casey questioned body counts, asked for number of Americans killed or wounded, and demanded proof the Pacification Program was working. Not the sort of questions the military was used to or ready to answer. Most reporters were older men and had supported the military during World War II and Korea, many earning their spurs there.

Walking alongside the general was Harry of the *Herald*, an ardent supporter of this war and a believer that all women should be home, barefoot, and pregnant. Harry had made that clear at his and Casey's first meeting in the rooftop bar of the Carevelle Hotel. Harry had made his reputation promoting and advancing the cause of the military and lived off the corresponding perks.

Dumpy and sweaty-looking in his camouflage fatigues, and wearing a hat old enough to have been worn by the French at Dien Bien Phu, Harry stood in sharp contrast to the trim and fit Falcon, whose fatigues were tailored to his tall, lean figure; four black cloth stars on both collars. With his hawk-like face, closely cropped hair, and sunburned skin pulled tight over his skull, Falcon looked every bit the modern-day warrior. And Falcon did not condescend to her as Harry did, asking what a nice girl like her was doing over here. Absolutely not. To this general, Casey was just another reporter—with tendencies toward communism.

"Ready to go up, Miss Blackburn?" Falcon held several terrain photographs.

"Yes, sir." Casey hated herself for adding the "sir." Maybe it came from hanging around too many brass-shiners or perhaps from being the daughter of a first sergeant. Could respect for rank be passed genetically? Casey didn't think so. These days it was more likely to have the opposite effect, and she knew more than one son or daughter who had taken to the streets to demonstrate against daddy's war effort. All Casey's friends opposed this war; many worked to end it. But maybe, just maybe, publishing the truth about what was happening over here might change more minds than taking to the streets.

✳   ✳   ✳

He was the lone survivor of the morning ambush. His patrol had been hit before noon, and now, late in the afternoon, he was running for his life. Kim hated the heavy rocket they made him carry across the border every night, the rocket his army called an RPG, and last night had been one of the worst. The enemy had more than their usual number of patrols out, and his squad had failed to reach its objective. He was worn out with lugging the heavy rocket back and forth across the border, and none of his fellow squad members had offered to help, causing Kim to fall farther and farther behind. Falling behind had saved his life. The RPG had saved his life.

The men ahead of him had been laughing and joking—bunched up in the enemy's kill zone. What was there to worry about? The enemy never worked this side of the border. His squad was sauntering along, passing through an open space on its left and a hedgerow on its right, when a murderous fire exploded from the thicket. Suddenly it was as if Kim were watching a marionette show: men jerking to and fro, up and down, then being thrown across the trail like discarded puppets.

The last man in the kill zone turned to run but before he could slip away, bullets slammed into him, picking him up and throwing him across the trail to join his comrades. In a matter of seconds, a file of soldiers had been turned into a line of corpses, chests ripped open and heads blown off. Blood ran everywhere, out of mouths, chests, and backs, the bodies so riddled the uniforms turned scarlet. When one of the bodies twitched, a final Claymore mine exploded, ripping into the bodies with its seven hundred buckshot-size ball bearings. Arms and legs jerked spasmodically; heads exploded like melons off the back of a speeding truck.

The ambush was so unexpected that Kim continued down the trail toward it. Until now, the closest Kim had come to enemy fire was when the Americans heaved mortar rounds in his direction after he'd fired his rocket into one of their huge base camps. Even then he was gone well before they could fix his position.

Kim stopped and stared as the wind picked up the smell of cordite and blew it in his direction. He had never seen bodies chewed up like this before. The only thing he could think of was when he had toured a battle-field where the enemy had brought in their gunships, ripping people apart and leaving little for families to mourn.

Kim had been there trying to locate his brother, a member of the Party for almost two years. He found nothing. Later, Kim learned the bodies had been dragged away so the Americans could not count their victims. Now more bodies lined the trail ahead of him, and the smell of gunpowder brought him back to the here and now. Kim turned and ran down the trail as fast as possible, only force of habit keeping him from dropping the abominable rocket. A kilometer later, he felt safe enough to stop and catch his breath. Bad idea. He had time to remember the bodies: the blood, the arms, the heads . . . .

Kim's stomach turned over and he puked beside the trail. He retched, coughed, and wiped his face on his shirtsleeve, then looked behind him. No one was charging down the trail. There was nothing. No birds, no animals, no sounds from insects. Only the quiet. It was much too quiet.

He must keep moving! That turn in the trail, the wood line to his right, the stand of bamboo almost at his elbow. The enemy could be anywhere!

Steadying the RPG on his shoulder, Kim fled back across the border, returning to South Vietnam. This time there was no stopping him until he found a trail sheltered by the jungle canopy, one that would take him north, paralleling the border between South Vietnam and Cambodia and away from this place.

An hour later, Kim turned west on a trail paralleling the trail where his squad had been ambushed. He left Vietnam behind and recrossed the border into Cambodia. Usually that gave him a sense of relief, but now, with the Americans operating on both sides of the border, he didn't feel safe anywhere.

Kim stopped and looked behind him toward the unmarked border. Had his patrol stumbled onto the American invasion of Cambodia? Everyone at base camp talked about the day the Americans would finally cross the border. Now they had, and killed all his comrades. Kim resettled the metal tube with its bulbous nose on his shoulder and hurried down the trail. He had to return to the base camp and warn his people.

After hiking up a steep hill, Kim broke out of the jungle and immediately recognized the area. Crossing this ridge would expose him until the trail dropped back into the jungle. His battalion commander had warned his troops to avoid this trail during daylight hours. Colonel Gzap had told them to use the safer and sheltered east-west trail to the south, the trail where Kim's squad had been obliterated.

He let out a sick little laugh. How could this trail be any more dangerous? He shifted the rocket to his other shoulder and started up the ridge.

Why had he done that? What good would it do to move the rocket? Both shoulders had been rubbed raw, and the cloth Kim used to cushion the rocket on his shoulder had been lost in his mad dash out of the Americans' ambush.

Kim rolled his shoulders. He wanted to stop and put the rocket down. His thighs ached, there was a pain in his side, and he had to force himself to put one foot in front of the other. But he must keep moving. He had to cross this ridge and reach the safety of the base camp in the valley below. In the base camp were tunnels, and everyone knew the Americans, even with their weapons, could not reach you inside a tunnel.

He glanced at a ridge running parallel to the one he was crossing. It, too, was totally bare. From there anyone could shoot him, and he would be just as dead as the rest of his squad. All an American soldier would have to do was adjust for distance, and there was little of that across the narrow valley.

Kim glanced down. A stream flowed between the ridges and sunlight bounced off the water, making it sparkle. The water came from the mountains but looked cool and refreshing, as if just beginning its journey downstream.

Kim's throat was parched, his clothing soaked, clinging to him. How long since he had had a drink of water? A drink of cool, refreshing water? At that creek. And that creek had been back across the border. He checked the sun's position. It had been over an hour since he had drunk any water and it would take him another hour to reach base camp.

Glancing at the stream below him, Kim stumbled. The rocket slipped off his shoulder, bounced on the edge of the cliff, and rolled over the side. Kim almost tumbled after it, but saved himself by windmilling his arms around.

May his ancestors preserve him! He was safe. But the rocket was gone!

Looking down, Kim expected to see the rocket falling into the valley below, but the rocket hung by its firing mechanism in a bush only two or three meters away, the barrel pointing at him accusingly. Colonel Gzap had cut off the little finger of the last man who had lost an RPG. Kim shivered in the afternoon sun. He didn't want to lose a finger.

There was little time to lose. He had to return to base camp and he had to have that rocket. Kim double-checked the far ridge, the tree line behind him, and then sat down and scooted over the side. There was just enough room above the bush for his feet. Below that, a sheer drop-off led to the cursed stream below.

Kim slid down the side of the ridge, planted his feet, and reached for the rocket.

Careful now. Take the rocket firmly.

He stretched out . . . but the rocket was out of reach. By millimeters. He tried again . . . again . . . but failed to . . . .

Oh, no! He had stretched too far! He was headed over the side! Hold on! Hold on! Dig in! Get a hold of something! Grab something!

Kim threw his hands back and clawed at the hill. His fingers scraped across a rock before finding ground they could dig into. Kim pulled back and flattened against the hill, chest pounding, legs weak, sweat running down his face. He had almost gone over the side and joined his ancestors.

Calm down.

There was no response from his foolish body. It continued to tremble.

This is an order. You must calm down!

His body refused to listen.

"Calm down!" he said to no one but himself. There is no way you will be able to grasp the rocket with shaking hands, and you must have that rocket.

Below, the water mocked him. Only last week Colonel Gzap had lectured them about giving in to weaknesses of the flesh. Leave that to the Americans, he had said, a people who carried more food than a family could eat in a whole week and listened to radios while on patrol. Kim found it hard to believe that Colonel Gzap would give into anything or anyone, even Party politicians from the North.

Kim stared at the rocket. Between him and the bush was nothing but the ledge made by his feet and that gave him an idea. He climbed back up on the ridge, lay on his stomach, and scooted over the side, using his hands to brake himself as he went down the face. When he thought he was within reach, he planted his left hand against the rock and scratched out notches with his toes to anchor him from above. Kim stretched out . . . and touched the rocket's nose.

But there was no way he could pull the rocket loose. The cursed thing was really stuck in that bush. Kim twisted the nose back and forth, but the rocket would not budge.

Would it explode? One had flown off his shoulder and landed in a hedgerow when all he had been doing was walking along, minding his own business. Now that had been a surprise, and caused him no end of explaining. It was also why his squad preferred he walk behind them—several meters behind them, his weapon pointed away from their formation.

Kim shook the cylinder, trying to break it free from the . . . .

Whump-whump-whump.

What was that sound? Was the rocket about to detonate?

Whump-whump-whump.

No. Kim knew that sound. It was the sound of an approaching helicopter. An American helicopter.

He looked up. There were three of them, flying on line and heading for his position. The Americans had waited until he was spread-eagled over the side of the cliff before showing themselves.

CHAPTER TWO

C asey held onto the sides of the Huey's open door and leaned out into the wind. Closing her eyes she could imagine herself hurtling down a highway on a motorcycle, which brought back memories of a fellow she'd probably never see again: a biker with the Hell's Angels.

The wind whipped through her fatigues but couldn't reach her hair tucked up under her flight helmet. The helmet had earphones on each side and a small microphone in front of her mouth. Through it she could communicate with anyone in the chopper. There were two pilots forward, and in the open bay with her was Falcon, his aide, and Harry of the *Herald*.

Falcon pointed at the jungle stretching out for miles: solid green with the odd splash of purple here and there. Casey could see his lips move, but his voice came through her helmet.

"There's a battalion-size base camp across that border, Miss Blackburn."

Casey looked over the sea of green but saw nothing. How could she? Three layers of canopy shielded her from the jungle floor. She hung on tight, leaned out, and looked for some sign of the base camp. She was trying to keep an open mind about this, but a battalion? A thousand people could be down there if Charlie had his family and political cadre with him.

Falcon made no bones about wanting to invade Cambodia, and flyovers like these were another part of his sales pitch, as much as the infrared photographs he had shown Casey before lifting off. He said they proved the base camp was there. Casey didn't doubt the photographs, but where'd they been taken? Over Cambodia or on another flyover, say, over North Vietnam?

"If I had a free hand, Miss Blackburn, I could clean out those sanctuaries and there wouldn't be a communist left in all Cambodia."

"Then Charlie would disappear into Laos and you'd want a free hand to go in there, then Burma, and before long you'd be fighting this war in India."

"Where do you want me to stop communism? Here or in San Francisco?"

All Casey could do was shake her head. As usual Falcon seemed absolutely sincere when reeling off his maxims. There must be a special class at West Point for teaching such pigheadedness and self-righteousness.

No. That wasn't right. You didn't have to attend The Point to absorb that philosophy. Her father had been just as adamant, and he had been an enlisted man.

"It would save a lot of American lives," stated Falcon.

"It didn't do anything for my father."

"But unlike you, KC believed in this war. Your father died for your right to question your country's role over here."

Casey knew everyone had heard her dressing-down via the Huey's on-board radio network. Heat rushed up the sides of her neck as she spat out, "Someone has to remind the generals there're real people down there, real people fighting and dying. Something generals tend to forget while being ferried around in helicopters."

She looked out the door and hung on tight, swaying with the motion of the chopper and staring at the gunship flying beside them. Unlike the Huey's pilots, the pilot of the Cobra sat behind the gunner, making their aircraft about a yard wide and giving the enemy next to nothing as a target. Like every other gunship, this one had that silly red face and razor-sharp teeth painted on its nose. If the damn thing could turn on a dime and come at you with machine guns firing and rockets blazing, why paint that stupid face on its nose? And why did this general encourage such behavior?

The Huey flew over the first of two ridges breaking up the jungle canopy. A stream cut through the valley and sunlight bounced off the water, making it sparkle. All very pleasing to the eye, but if this was all there was to see, she was ready to return to Long Bien where she could dig up a real story. Around any base camp there were GIs willing to talk or complain, especially to a woman from back home, and that's how she'd gotten a good number of leads. Matter of fact, there was a soldier who'd said he'd show her . . . .

Was someone down there? On the far ridge? Casey hung on, leaned out, and looked again. She thought she'd seen someone, a figure scurrying up the side of the ridge.

Casey turned to tell Falcon what she'd seen but changed her mind. No, sirree, she would not tell this man anything. Earlier in the flight, they'd laughed at her for thinking she had seen something on the ground. She'd be damned if she'd give them another chance to laugh at her again. She'd hang on and see if these men could see what she saw.

On the ridge, Kim forgot all about the rocket's instability, reached down, and snatched the cylinder out of the bush. He scooted up the ridge on his chest and scrambled to his feet. Dirt fell from the blouse of his uniform, and he removed a twig from the firing mechanism as he glanced at the tree line fifty meters away. The base camp was twice that far down the other side of the ridge.

Whump-whump-whump.

The Americans were over the valley, seconds away from attack. There were four helicopters, not three: two Hueys, one behind the other, and flanking the lead Huey, two gunships. Cobras. He was a dead man. But this time he would not run. Earlier today he had, but not this time. This time he would stand and fight. He would make his ancestors proud. Kim shouldered his rocket, raised the sight, and fired.

He missed. The rocket flew past the Huey and through its blades. One of the rotor blades caught the

17

rocket's tail, clipping off a sizable piece of blade. The rocket detonated, but only after falling to the ground on the other side of the border. By then Kim was racing for the tree line.

Inside the Huey, one of Casey's hands jerked loose as she was thrown backwards when the helicopter suddenly lurched to one side. As the pilot pulled back on the stick, righting the chopper but overcompensating for the tilt, Casey's other hand lost its grip and she was thrown in the opposite direction and out the open door.

Falcon, who always said the only way to ride a chopper was with spongy legs and a tight right hand, caught Casey as she flew past. Her arm slipped through his hand until his fingers clamped down on her wrist. She screamed as the jungle leaped up in her face.

The pilot righted the chopper, causing Casey to be shoved toward the Huey's open bay, where Falcon pulled her back inside. Casey planted her feet, grabbed the overhead and nodded her thanks. She hung on and tried to catch her breath. She trembled. Her legs felt weak.

Suddenly the Huey rolled over on its side, and though Casey was ready for it, her legs went flying out the door again. Below her, the jungle rolled and pitched like an angry sea. The chopper shifted again, and Casey was thrown back inside, her feet slamming to the metal deck. That hurt! But not as much as the burning in her shoulders. The Huey was playing crack the whip, every snap almost jerking her arms out of their sockets.

"There's damage to the blades." The pilot's voice came through everyone's headset. "She's out of balance."

Tell me about it! Some strange force seemed to have seized the ship and was shaking the bejesus out of it. Casey was going to be sick, throwing up what little breakfast she'd eaten.

"Mayday! Mayday!" The copilot's voice sounded remarkably calm as the helicopter rolled and pitched. "Eagle's Nest, this is Falcon One. Mayday! Mayday!"

My God! Were they going down?

Casey stared at the miles and miles of green that stretched to the horizon.

Oh, no! Not down there!

"We've got to get in those seats!" shouted Falcon.

The general hung on with one hand, the other tight on the belt of Casey's fatigues. He gestured with his head toward the nylon seat belts attached to aluminum seats against the rear bulkhead.

Casey stared at the seats only a few feet away. They might as well have been back in Long Bien. "I'll take my chances here!"

"That's no chance at all! You'll be thrown out on impact!"

"Get in those seats!" came the voice of the pilot through their headsets. "We're going down!"

Casey glanced around the empty cabin. "Where's Harry and your aide?"

"They're gone!"

"*Gone???*"

The general nodded grimly.

That did it! Let this chopper shake, rattle, and roll.

She wasn't going anywhere.

Kim cursed himself as he raced for the trees. Instead of running he should stand and die. He had missed the American helicopter, and earlier today he had stood by as his squad was destroyed. Twice in the same day he'd disgraced his family. He deserved to die and be buried in an unmarked grave. Still, he ran for the safety of the tree line.

The miles and miles of green had lulled the gunship pilots into a dulled state. They weren't aware anything was wrong until Kim's rocket hit the ground. They looked from the explosion to the general's Huey swaying back and forth and heading across the border . . . into Cambodia.

"What the hell . . . ?" muttered one of them.

As they watched, the Huey rolled over on its side.

"What's going on?"

"Falcon One took a hit!"

"What?"

"I repeat: Falcon took a hit."

"From where?"

"From the valley—no! Look! On the ridge!"

"It's Charlie! You're closer. Get him! I'll follow."

"Can't! Already over him. Got to come around."

"Orbit right. I've got the dink heading for the tree line."

The ridge was sprayed with machine-gun fire; then there was silence on the net as the two gunships evaluated the results.

"You missed," said the pilot who had orbited right.

"Come around! Try again! Before he gets into the trees."

"You see him?"

"He's closing with the trees, but I've got him!"

"Use your rockets. Knock the son of a bitch down! Keep him where we can see him."

A rocket exploded on the far ridge.

"Got him! Got him!"

"Can you see the body?"

"Not with all the smoke."

Kim was alive but down. The rocket had exploded behind him, lifting him up, and throwing him toward the trees. He didn't know it, but shrapnel had pierced his thigh, an arm, and his head, literally scalping hair off one side. Dazed, he sat up and looked around.

Kim couldn't understand what was happening, but it seemed awfully important to reach the tree line. He would be safer under the trees. Trees had hidden his ancestors for generations. He stood up, and the world— a silent one—spun around. He stepped forward and tripped over a log. Landing hard, he raised his head and looked at the log.

Where had that come from? Using his hands and knees, he took several steps and went down on his face. The jolt reminded him of why he had been running for the trees.

American helicopters were after him! Cobras!

Through the smoke, he saw the narrow-faced monsters, teeth dripping blood, ready to devour him. Losing control, Kim wet himself. He jammed himself alongside the log as the Cobras raked the ridge with machine-gun fire.

"Smoke or no smoke, that should've gotten the little bastard!"

"But where's the body?" asked the other pilot after making another pass over the ridge.

"Look! Eleven o'clock. That's him!"

"No! That's a log!"

"He's slipped into the woods. Quick! Take their tops off!"

"Wilco!"

Rockets exploded and the sky rained leaves, limbs, and splinters. Kim covered his head with his hands and squeezed in against the log. Feeling had returned to his limbs . . . his voice, too. He begged for mercy and promised to live a more righteous life if his ancestors would only save him.

When the Cobras completed their pass, Kim shook the debris off and looked up. The trees were still there, but their tops were gone. The Americans had ripped his cover away! Now they could see him inside the tree line. And the choppers were circling for another run. He had to find a place to hide—and quick!

Kim tried to stand, but the world whirled around in muffled silence. He didn't hear himself hit the ground—only felt it. What to do? He could not run and there was no place to hide. Kim grabbed a piece of wood that had splintered off the log and started hollowing out a hole beside the log. But what was he hollowing out—a hiding place or a grave?

The soldiers in Kim's base camp looked toward the ridge. When the gun and rocket runs didn't stop, each glanced around, making sure he knew the location of his weapon and the entrance to the nearest tunnel.

"What is happening up there?" asked a short, squat Vietnamese with thick arms sticking out of a dull green military blouse. He wore the standard NVA pith helmet and stared in the direction of the ridge, a kilometer of jungle away and up a steep hill.

"Sounds like American gunships attacking someone on the ground," said Colonel Gzap, strolling out of the command hut, a building made of wood and roofed with thatch.

"But it is against the Americans' rules of engagement to cross the border."

Gzap flashed one of his rare smiles. His first sergeant's sense of order was being violated. "Put the camp on alert and send two of our best runners up there."

"Yes, sir!"

"Then mobilize Bien's platoon. Send it up there also. And make sure Bien has a working radio."

The first sergeant grimaced. A working radio was not the easiest thing to find, even in a base camp the size of theirs. The first sergeant called out some names and two boys rushed around the corner of the hut. They glanced at Gzap as they came to a halt.

The sergeant snapped out their orders, and off the boys ran, through the camp and up the trail. In thirty minutes, one of them would return with a full report. The other boy would stay behind to relate any further action.

Gzap watched the boys go. They reminded him of how he had gotten his start against the French, becoming a runner the day after the French had shot his village chief. That man had also been his father—shot in front of not only his family but the entire village.

"Prepare to move underground!" shouted the first sergeant.

Gzap left the alerting of the base camp to his subordinate and reentered the command hut. Aides came to attention as he crossed the dirt-floored room. The colonel never saw them. He had eyes only for the map. When he looked at a map, Gzap could almost feel what was happening out there.

His first sergeant was correct. The Americans should not have crossed the border. For some reason they considered Cambodia neutral. What nonsense! When the reunification of your country was at stake, no place could be neutral. Gzap fished a cigarette out of his pocket and ran his finger along the path to the ridge. Now why would the Americans be firing up there?

In the air over the ridge, confusion reigned among the gunship pilots.

"Where's the damn gook!"

"Can't see. Too much smoke."

"He's down there somewhere. There's no way he could've gotten off that ridge."

"He's dead."

"Roger that, but we'll still neutralize the area up to twenty-five meters into the tree line. I'm going hot with my forty mike-mikes."

"Wilco."

Both gunships passed over the ridge and let loose with their forty millimeter grenade launchers.

Kim huddled under the log and shuddered and shook as the ridge was hosed down by the attacking Cobras. Rockets exploded around him, ripping up the ground. One landed on the other side of the log, shoving it on top of him. Kim tried to get his breath. Instead, he got a mouthful of gunpowder. He screamed until the ground stopped shaking.

"He's dead. No one could survive that."

"Guess not," replied the second pilot.

"You guess not? Want to land down there and search for the body?"

"Nah. Like you said. He's dead."

"You're damn right he's dead. Now let's—oh, my God! Look at Falcon's chopper."

In the cabin of the helicopter, Falcon had gotten one hand on the metal tubing forming the base of the harness seat. When he was fully extended, one hand there, the other still over the door, the chopper lurched again. His and Casey's feet went flying out the door.

Casey's legs felt weak, her stomach hollow, but her shoulders worried her most. They burned with pain. Still, Falcon seemed as calm as when making a presentation at the Five O'Clock Follies—which Casey might never again attend!

Over the sound of the wind blowing through the open

door, Falcon shouted, "When we get back inside, jump for the seat! I'll catch you."

Casey shook her head violently. She didn't want to end up like Harry and Falcon's aide. No, sirree, she wasn't going to jump for anything. Glancing down, Casey saw the jungle rushing toward her.

"Get set!" shouted the pilot. "We're going down!"

The chopper righted itself, Casey's feet slammed into the deck, and she leaped for the seat—and missed. The roar of the engine drowned out her screams as she flew across the open bay.

Falcon was ready for her. Holding onto the base of the webbed-back chair, he let go his hand holding onto the side of the Huey's open hatch and swung around behind her. He followed Casey across the cabin and knocked her down. After slamming the girl facedown to the metal deck, he grabbed the base on the other side of the chair. There, he straddled her until the girl realized she was still inside the helicopter. Looking up, Casey grabbed the chair and burst into tears.

"No time for that! Get in that seat!"

Casey nodded and pushed herself up between his arms and into his face. The general made way, letting Casey slide her head, then her shoulders, and finally her bottom between his arms and past his face. She reached out and got a hand into the webbing of the seat but could go no further. The helicopter was headed for the ground and it felt like she was climbing straight up. She wanted to let go and stop the burning in her arms.

When Falcon noticed the woman had stopped moving, he fought back a surge of panic. The helicopter was losing altitude fast, the jungle ready to devour them. "Get up there, Casey!"

"I can't!"

"Do it, lady!" Falcon reared back his head and cracked his helmet across her rump.

Casey sobbed, put one hand ahead of the other, and finished her climb. She took a moment to catch her breath, then turned around to sit down. The only way she could take a seat was if Falcon held onto the webbing and pulled himself up into her, forcing her body into the seat.

Falcon fought inertia as the chopper hurled itself toward the ground. His arms ached, the left one hyperextended from catching the girl when she'd almost gone out the door, and he didn't dare look out those doors. He just might lose his nerve.

Casey pulled the belt around her and closed the buckle with a snap. Falcon grabbed for his seat and got his hands into the webbing. He was twisting around and sitting down when the chopper crashed through the first layer of the jungle canopy.

CHAPTER THREE

O ver the jungle roof the pilot of the second Huey, call sign "Westwood," watched in horror as his commanding officer's chopper disappeared into the jungle below. After the Huey disappeared, no hole or gap remained in the jungle roof, no torn treetops . . . no nothing.

Westwood blinked. Where'd it gone? A helicopter couldn't just disappear without a trace.

But this one had.

"My God! Did you see that?" asked his copilot.

Shouts of "May Day" and the location of the crashing chopper, mixed with a woman's screams, still rang in the pilot's ears. But now the net was silent. Absolutely quiet.

Westwood hovered over the jungle roof, waiting for Falcon's chopper to mark its location by exploding fuel tanks. As Westwood waited, he shot a nervous glance in the direction of the NVA base camp. Wouldn't it be better if Falcon were killed outright than if he were captured by the North Vietnamese?

Captured by the North Vietnamese? What the hell was he thinking? You couldn't consider the possibility. Falcon was the commander of not only all American forces in Vietnam but also troops from several other countries that had sent men to Southeast Asia.

"We've got to pop smoke," shouted one of the door gunners from the rear of the chopper. The soldier was strapped in behind a machine gun that pointed out the open door. Across the bay sat a similar soldier, machine gun pointed out the open hatch.

The door gunner was right. They had to drop canisters of smoke into the jungle—make that red smoke in all this green—or risk losing Falcon's location forever.

Westwood broke out of his holding pattern and took his chopper down for a look-see, practically turning the Huey on its nose. He saw nothing. The roof was a sheet of green. The jungle had swallowed the chopper whole.

"What're you doing?" screamed the door gunner. "This isn't the spot! You've got to go back across the border!"

"What the hell are you talking about?" demanded Westwood. "I saw where the chopper went down!"

"Turn this bird around! I know where Falcon is! To the left." The door gunner glanced at a low hill to the west which carried the odd name of Magic Mountain. "To the south, I mean. Hurry before I lose his position."

"Both of you are wrong," chimed in the copilot. "You

have to go east another klick. The CIC did not crash in Cambodia."

The pilot stared at his opposite number. Go east another thousand yards? Had the man lost his mind? But his copilot wasn't looking at him. He was watching a canister of red smoke on its way toward the jungle roof. The door gunner had made the decision for all of them.

"What the hell are you doing, Lancaster?"

"Popping smoke, sir."

"And just who the hell told you to do that?"

"We didn't want to lose Falcon's position, sir."

Westwood stared into the jungle: miles and miles of green in every direction. Hell, without an explosion to mark Falcon's location, one place was as good as another.

"How many smokes you got back there, Lancaster?"

"Not enough, sir."

When Kim was sure the firing had stopped, he dug himself out of his hole and shoved the log off. Tunnels he could stand but being crushed to death by a cursed log was another matter. He gasped for breath, pulled himself up, and grabbed the other side of the log. Its surface was rough to the touch, chewed up from the rounds fired by the gunships.

Kim could not stop shaking and continued to grasp the log as if it were a lifeline to another reality. Through the smoke, he saw the Americans returning to Vietnam. Suddenly, one of their helicopters rolled over on its side and plunged into the jungle. Kim held his breath and waited, then stood on shaking legs, one hand holding onto the roughened wood.

The Huey failed to resurface. The metal bird had crashed into the jungle. The Americans would never see that helicopter again. Kim had been a member of search parties. If you found anything in the jungle, it was strictly luck.

Kim slid to his knees beside the log and dropped his head as he said a prayer of thanks. It was true what the old ones of his village said. The dead could reach out of their graves and lend a hand to younger generations. Today was proof of that.

When the North Vietnamese first sergeant returned to the command hut, a corporal was packing away their gear for the move into the tunnels, and Colonel Gzap was still at his map, puffing away on another cigarette. One butt already lay on the ground at his feet. The map was nailed to a support beam and covered with a piece of plastic, plastic used by Americans to ship artillery rounds. Gzap traced the trail from his base camp up to and across the ridge. Then his finger crossed the border into South Vietnam. Gzap pulled his finger back to the higher ground as several of his staff rushed into the hut, straightening blouses and snatching off pith helmets.

They gathered around Gzap. A corporal stuck his hand through the group standing in front of the map and marked the estimated position of the runners who had left base camp only five minutes before. The corporal returned to his seat and studied his wristwatch.

As the minutes passed, he ticked them off on a scrap of paper, occasionally glancing at other scraps of paper lying around him on the dirt floor.

Gzap took a grease pencil from the breast pocket of his fatigue blouse and drew a circle around the spot where Kim was celebrating his victory over the American Huey. Gzap tapped the map with his pencil. "Here."

"But how do you know?" asked the newest member of his staff.

The first sergeant grimaced. The boy was the son of a prominent Hanoi politician. Ever since arriving in camp, he had subjected everyone, including Gzap, to the most rudimentary questions. The first sergeant couldn't decide whether the boy was an inept spy for the Party or simply another green officer.

Gzap continued to stare at the map. "I know this is the location because it is about how far the sound of a rocket might carry under the triple canopy, and the only area an American gunship might spot any ground activity." The colonel stepped back. "But what kind of activity? What is happening up there?"

Gzap was talking to himself, and his staff knew better than to interrupt. The green lieutenant did not. "The Americans have crossed the border!"

With the exception of Gzap, everyone glanced in the direction of the ridge, then at a soldier passing equipment to another through a hole in the floor. It was the entrance to the executive tunnel where Gzap and his staff might hide, and not much different from any other tunnel in the base camp.

"No. If the Americans had invaded Cambodia, we

would have had advance warning from our people in the Presidential Palace in Saigon." Gzap tapped the map, then took a drag of his cigarette. "Who do we have up there, First Sergeant?"

Members of the staff who were huddled around the map made way for the stubby man. "That is what is so puzzling, sir. No one should be there. That trail is off-limits during daylight hours."

"Are we expecting anyone from Vietnam?"

"No, sir."

"Defectors?"

"Not ARVNs. Soldiers of the Army of the Republic of Vietnam," said the sergeant with a snort, "do not desert but go home to their mothers."

Smiles broke out all around, but no one laughed, save the green lieutenant. He did not laugh long.

"Who of our people has not reported in?"

A major stepped to the map. "We have only one over-due patrol and it is doubtful they would be that far north." He pointed at the east-west trail. "This was their assigned trail."

Gzap lit another cigarette from the one he was smoking, then dropped the butt to the floor, snubbing it out under his boot.

"They got lost," suggested the new lieutenant.

"No," said Gzap, shaking his head. "Everyone knows his way home. It is the first thing you learn in the jungle, and something that does not have to be taught."

"Besides," explained the first sergeant, "there are not enough radios for units to leave their assigned trails. They could be mistaken for the enemy." The sergeant wanted more radios and knew this boy's father could get them. The little pain in the butt might as well be useful for something.

Gzap was still staring at his map. "We have lost several patrols out there . . . I think the lurps are responsible."

"Lurps?" asked the green lieutenant.

"American long-range reconnaissance patrols—sent out to spy on us."

"Their time is short," said another member of the staff. "Soon we will find and destroy them."

Gzap wasn't so sure. How did you protect your men from an enemy who initiated contact only when it was to their advantage, an enemy who could disappear at a moment's notice because there were so few of them and they traveled so lightly? No. The only way you could stop a team of lurps would be if they stood and fought, and lurps never stood and fought.

"Call coming in, sir."

Everyone turned to the radiotelephone operator, an older man who sat at a table covered with radios, headsets, and microphones left behind when the French had pulled out of Vietnam.

"These men," said the RTO, "a Viet Cong patrol, are on the east-west trail." He paused, a puzzled look crossing his face. "They think a helicopter crashed near their position."

Gzap was across the room before the mouths of his staff finished falling open. If there was fighting on the ridge to the east of them . . . and a helicopter had gone down out there . . . it could only mean . . . .

He snatched the headset off the RTO and picked up a microphone. "Identify yourself."

The squad leader on the east-west trail did so.

"What is this about a helicopter?" Gzap knew he had to be careful. With Viet Cong, you had to give a lot to get a little. And they, for some reason, had a radio.

"I am not sure—we are not sure, sir. We think we heard a crash . . . just north of the trail. From the noise it had to have torn a hole in the canopy. Perhaps a helicopter."

"Any explosions?"

"No, sir. Not yet."

"What are your coordinates?"

The Viet Cong squad leader read off some letters that Gzap repeated for his aide to translate and post on the map.

"Sundown at seventeen-thirty-two, sir," the young man said before turning to the task of converting the letters to latitude and longitude on a slip of paper.

Gzap nodded. It was always dusk under the triple canopy, and in a couple of hours it would be dark as night.

To the man on the east-west trail, Gzap said, "Assemble on line and sweep north. Before you leave the trail, make sure your men are at least five meters apart but always maintaining visual contact. Do you have a compass?"

"Yes, sir, I do."

"Place yourself in the middle of the sweep. Plot an azimuth and stay on it. If an American helicopter has crashed out there, I want it found, and before dark."

"Yes, sir."

"Are you wearing the radio?"

"Er—no, sir."

"Put it on. I want to be in contact with you at all times. Do you get all that?"

"Yes, sir."

"Then repeat it back to me."

It took a minute, but the squad leader finally got it right.

After signing off, Gzap handed the headset to a major instead of the radiotelephone operator. "Monitor this frequency. I want to know the moment anything comes in."

The major nodded and put the headset on. At the same time Gzap's young aide posted the location of the squad on the east-west trail. The position was well south of the noise from the ridge, and just inside the Cambodian border.

Gzap returned to the map and fired up another cigarette as he watched the young man update the position of the runners on their way to the ridge. "Is Bien's platoon ready to move out?"

"Knowing Bien, sir, it probably has."

Gzap ran his finger up and down the trail running south from his base camp. When the trail reached a hill called Magic Mountain, it continued south, but also connected with an east-west trail, the trail where the Viet Cong were searching for the so-called helicopter.

"Change of orders, First Sergeant." Gzap tapped the east-west trail where the Viet Cong were beginning their sweep. "I want Bien here, backing up the Viet Cong at the crash site. And tell him I want him there immediately."

"Yes, sir." The first sergeant disappeared out the door of the command hut.

"Sir," said the major monitoring the Viet Cong squad with the headset. He tried to leave the table but the wire connecting the headset to the radio did not allow much movement. He gestured at the map. "There should be a squad moving toward the Viet Cong's location. Coming in from the west. Right, Corporal?"

The aide looked up from where he sat, cross-legged, on the dirt floor. "Yes, sir, that is correct." He glanced at the clipboard lying across his lap. "A sapper squad crossing into Vietnam to blow bridges."

"Radio?" asked Gzap.

"No, sir."

Gzap muttered a curse. There were always plenty of men, but never enough radios. "Tell that Viet Cong squad on the east-west trail to be on the lookout for the sappers approaching from the direction of Magic Mountain. I would not want them to mistake each other for the enemy."

The major nodded, then relayed the information to the east-west trail. He told the squad leader to fire his rifle once he returned to the trail, a sure sign that friendlies were in the area.

"I still want a platoon on that ridge." Gzap pointed to the trail that crossed the ridge and returned to South Vietnam. "Once they check the ridge, have that platoon move into South Vietnam, then south on the trail that intersects the east-west trail." Where Gzap pointed, the east-west trail entered Vietnam.

"This second platoon is to establish a blocking position along the border and stop any survivors from returning to Vietnam. Have them cover one full kilometer in either direction of the east-west trail. If there are any Americans out there, I intend to have them."

CHAPTER FOUR

The popping of smoke by the Westwood chopper broke the silence in the command bunker back in Long Bien, the nerve center for all American operations in South Vietnam. The military personnel had been collectively holding their breath and staring at the speaker over the huge map of South Vietnam at the far end of the room. The map hung there, as the speaker did, giving the illusion that the command center was in touch with the field.

This couldn't be happening!

But it was. It had already happened. In a country without front lines, the CIC's chopper had gone down behind enemy lines!

They had to get Falcon out of there, and they had to get him out fast! They couldn't let Charlie capture their CO. How would they explain that to the president? To the American people? Oh, God, just wait until the press got hold of this!

Several officers hustled over to the map. Based on what they'd heard over the command net and knowing the CIC's flight plan, they began arguing over where, exactly, Falcon One had gone down. Other officers rushed to the noncoms sitting at the communications console and tried to use one of the many radiotelephones.

It was impossible. Other commanders had the same idea—in the field or not—and the command net became jammed, worse than useless. Static and screech roared through the speaker at the far end of the room. No one was listening to anyone and everyone had something to say. Enlisted men glanced nervously at each other. The command center for all US forces in South Vietnam was in chaos.

A bald master sergeant had seen enough. He pushed his way through the double doors and rushed down the hallway to the officers' mess. Overcome by the moment, the sergeant almost shouted as he came through the door to the mess hall. He pulled up short when he saw Colonel Daniels, the officer of the day, having a cup of coffee with an officer who had served under Daniels during his last assignment.

The younger officer, Captain Manley, was saying, "Now that my ticket's punched over here, it's off to the Career Course."

"But you'll be back," said Colonel Daniels with a small smile.

"Oh, yes, I'll be back," Manley said, smiling himself. "More than one tour in 'Nam always looks good on one's record."

"Maybe they'll give you this job," said Daniels, still smiling.

Knowing the responsibilities of the officer of the day, technically responsible for anything that occurred on a twenty-four-hour watch, Manley laughed. "Then I'd rather not return at all."

They noticed the master sergeant gripping both sides of the door and leaning into the mess area. It was a small room with few tables; a central kitchen area served officers on one side, enlisted men on the other.

"Yes, Harmon?" asked Daniels.

Harmon glanced at Manley. "Er—sir, well . . . we could use you in the command center."

The OD's eyes twinkled. "Captain Manley has the proper clearances."

"Er—I hope so." Harmon scanned the room as he hurried over to the table. Running through his head was the old World War II slogan: Loose Lips Sink Ships, and Harmon didn't want to be part of any sinking of the commanding general. Bending over the table, he said in a low voice, "Falcon One's gone down on the other side of the border. In Cambodia."

Daniels stood up, knocking over his coffee. The brownish liquid washed across the surface of the table. "Are you serious?"

"I'm afraid so, sir."

"Is this some kind of a drill?"

"No, sir. Absolutely not!"

"Is he . . . alive?" asked Manley. The younger man's voice cracked, his tanned face suddenly pale.

"We don't know, sir."

"Radio out?" asked Daniels.

"We assume so."

"Let's hope that's what it is." The OD strode out of the room and down the hall with Harmon and Manley on his heels. "Do we have a location?"

Harmon gave it to him.

"Isn't that close to that NVA base camp?"

"Yes, sir. Falcon took some reporters to see it."

"Now I understand why his staff doesn't like those damn flyovers."

Harmon followed the OD through the doors of the command bunker. Manley came in behind them, unnoticed by the sergeant posted at the door. Captain Manley didn't have proper clearance for this area, but he wouldn't miss this for all the world.

Colonel Daniels strode through the confusion and stepped up on the platform where the radiotelephone operators were trying to handle the incoming calls. Everybody and his brother were trying to contact the command bunker, demanding to know what Long Bien was going to do about Falcon. Many had their own suggestions.

Daniels glanced at the speaker over the map at the other end of the underground room. Whatever was on the command net couldn't be heard for all the commotion. Clusters of uniformed personnel here and there were engaging in heated discussions and gesturing at the map of South Vietnam at the far end of the room.

"Group . . . attention!" shouted Manley.

Chairs screeched across the floor and clusters of men stopped their conversations as soldiers scrambled to their feet, becoming ramrod straight. In the silence, Daniels could hear the distortion on the command net.

"Which one of these phones is mine?" the OD asked the nearest radiotelephone operator.

The soldier stuck out a stiff hand from his position of attention. "That one, sir!"

"Be at ease." Daniels glanced at the man's name tag. "Sparkman, switch to the alternate frequency. Let's see if anyone at the crash site had the good sense to do the same."

"Stand . . . at ease!" shouted Master Sergeant Harmon before Captain Manley could upstage him again.

Feet slid apart, hands were slapped behind backs, and heads snapped around to watch the officer of the day at the communications console. Soldiers didn't obtain jobs in the command center without a strong sense of military protocol—and curiosity.

Radiotelephone operator Sparkman punched up the alternate frequency and a voice from the trail Huey broke the relative calm of the command bunker. Heads snapped around again, this time staring at the speaker over the huge map displaying the army's four corps operating in South Vietnam.

". . . come in, dammit! Where the hell are you, Long Bien?"

Daniels picked up his phone and spoke into it so softly that the master sergeant could hear the OD better over the speaker on the far wall. "Give me a situation report . . . once you've identified yourself."

"This is Westwood! Where the hell you been? I've

been on this alternate frequency forever. What you mean 'sit rep'? Falcon One just crashed into the goddamn jungle. It disappeared!"

"No reason for that kind of language on the net," Daniels went on softly. "Now what do you mean it's gone? What's the terrain out there?"

A skinny major was pointing at the spot on the map where the command center thought Falcon's chopper had gone down. Daniels recognized the area from one of his field tours, and his stomach went hollow.

"Triple canopy!" shouted Westwood. "That's where he disappeared! I'm over the site right now, and we popped smoke, but that's all we can see. Just a little trail of smoke . . . that's all that's left. A little smoke. There's no sign of where they went down. No hole in the canopy, no nothing." Westwood stopped to catch his breath. "If you can believe that."

Daniels believed. He'd worked under triple canopy before. "Pull yourself together, Westwood. You're my eyes out there. Was there any explosion?"

"No—thank God."

A little good news, thought the OD.

Another voice broke in on the alternate command net, demanding to know what the hell Long Bien was going to do about getting Falcon out of that damn jungle.

"Clear this net!" screamed Daniels. "The next man that comes on this net in an unauthorized manner will be brought up on charges. If that's clear give me a double click." An enormous number of double clicks were followed by Daniels asking, "Are the shooters on this frequency?"

"Yes, sir," came the quick and dual reply from the Cobra gunships.

"Split up and cover the area. Find Westwood a landing zone."

Over the crash site Westwood's heart sank. He didn't want to land. There could be a million Charlies down there. "Er—Eagles's Nest, this is Westwood. I have a hoist onboard."

"Then prepare for an insertion! The shooters might not find that LZ."

"Wilco! Westwood, out!"

Daniels looked to his air force liaison. "Put your Phantoms on alert."

"Already done, sir. Standing by for your command."

"Good. And send up a couple of planes for an infrared flyover, and more than one forward observer. I want some shots of the crash site before Falcon's chopper cools off." The air force colonel reached for his phone, but Daniels stopped him with, "Add to that a C-130 with the most sensitive communications equipment you have onboard, a Batcat over the crash site at all times."

The air force liaison nodded and reached for his phone. This one was shaping up to be a real bitch.

Daniels turned to Harmon. "Sergeant, send someone to the airstrip. Your best driver. I want those infrareds here as soon as those planes touch down."

"Yes, sir!" And Harmon barked at an E-6, sending him on the run through the double doors.

"What about maps?" asked Captain Manley from below the console. "Detailed blowups of the crash area?"

"Find them! If not here, call the spooks," said Daniels,

referring to the CIA. He didn't look at Manley but stared at a colonel across the room. "Cromley, call up your long-range reconnaissance patrols. See who they have in the area. We might get lucky. Then locate the nearest airborne unit. I want at least a company. Tell them to travel light and to be prepared to rappel over two hundred feet into the jungle."

Cromley nodded nervously. He'd never held a field command and he had been recently transferred in from Supply. His buddies told him that this would look good on his résumé, but what was happening was happening much too fast for Cromley. He turned to his RTO for assistance, but the officer of the day wasn't through yet.

"Cromley, send that airborne unit to the crash site, but there's to be no insertion except on my command."

The colonel nodded several times before turning back to his RTO.

Daniels had already forgotten about the man. The OD was staring at the information on a blackboard below the operational map on the front wall. Included in the weather forecast was sundown at 17:32. Daniels glanced at the clock over the map. Little less than two hours of daylight to find Falcon, if you could call what you found on the jungle floor daylight.

The officer of the day surveyed the command center. Things were coming together, but there were still too many people in here. Word traveled fast, and everyone wanted to be either a part of rescuing Falcon or watch how it was being done. It would be something to brag about at the "O" Club—which wouldn't be what the

Pentagon would want. The Pentagon would want damage control—and fast.

Daniels glanced at the double doors. The sergeant of the guard seemed more interested in what was going on inside the room than who might be sneaking in. "Harmon, clear this room! No more than the senior man and one aide at each post. Have the other personnel taken down to their respective mess areas, and get some MPs to hold them. Secure the command center, then the whole compound. Anyone can enter, but no one's to leave. Have all indigenous personnel removed from the compound immediately. By force if necessary. Refer all inquiries to me if you can't handle them."

"Yes, sir!" replied the master sergeant. "And I can handle it. Sir."

The OD glanced at the sergeant posted at the double doors. "And get someone else on the door!"

"Yes, sir!"

Turning to the row of RTOs at the communication center, Daniels asked, "What you got for me, Sparkman?"

"Jones is monitoring the old command net."

The OD looked down the line at the next RTO. "Heard anything, Jones?"

"Nothing, sir. Everybody must've wised up and switched frequencies. And there's nothing from Falcon's chopper. They're either dead or unconscious."

"Or his radio's out," Daniels added quickly. "Let's watch our tongues here. Where's the executive officer?"

"The usual, sir," Sparkman said. "Out with one of the pacification teams."

"Anyone tried to reach him?"

The row of RTOs shook their heads, but Sparkman said, "I have, sir, but I can't locate him."

"Have someone keep trying. I don't want to talk to him, just advise the XO of the situation. He'll get in here fast enough."

Sparkman turned to another soldier farther down the console. "Get the exec in here, Ozzimo."

Ozzimo glared at Sparkman, a soldier he outranked by more than one stripe.

Daniels saw the confrontation building. "Do as he says, Ozzimo. Sparkman outranks you and everyone on this console as of now. It's a field promotion. I don't have time for games."

Ozzimo muttered under his breath and punched up the executive officer's frequency.

"Sparkman, if Ozzimo doesn't cooperate, replace him, and fast. Anything else I should know?"

"Westwood's man's in the hoist."

"But will the hoist reach the jungle floor? It could be over two hundred feet from the top of the canopy to the floor."

Cradling the phone between head and shoulder, Sparkman gestured helplessly with open palms.

"Have someone find out! Anyone but you."

"Yes, sir!" Sparkman shouted the order down the console.

"Infrared over target in four minutes!" called out the air force liaison from his desk across the room.

"Sparkman, pull everyone back from the crash site. I don't want their engines distorting my pictures. And make sure they pop smoke before leaving. Plenty of it. I'll be damned if I'm going to lose that location." Daniels looked at the air force colonel. "You putting a reference point on those pictures for me?"

"SOP."

The OD nodded and turned to Cromley, who'd been asked to locate any long-range reconnaissance patrols near the crash site and to mobilize an airborne unit. "What you got for me, Cromley?"

The colonel covered the bottom of his phone and shook his head.

"What's that supposed to mean?"

"I—I'm not . . . they're not sure, sir."

Daniels looked down where Master Sergeant Harmon was insisting that Captain Manley leave the command center. "Manley, get over there and get what I need. ASAP!"

The captain shook loose of the master sergeant and ran over to the colonel's desk. He snatched the phone out of Cromley's hand.

Cromley stared at Manley as the junior officer screamed into the phone. Did he have to yell like that? Certainly the same results could be achieved without abusing the man on the other end of the line. Cromley glanced around. Everyone was so busy, moving or talking rapidly. Or both. Just watching them made him nervous. He glanced at his RTO. The man didn't even look at him. Probably intimidated by this fellow Manley, a rather common-looking man. They'd let anyone in the army when there was a war going on.

Cromley realized there were more than two men at

his post and remembered the order by Master Sergeant Harmon to clear the room. An enlisted man giving orders to officers. A bad precedent to set. Maybe he should go down to the officers' mess and see what was going on. Certainly it wouldn't be as hectic in there, and he might learn what others thought about how the officer of the day was going about the job of rescuing Falcon.

Sparkman waved a hand in front of Daniels. "Sir, it's a toss-up as to whether the hoist on Westwood's chopper will reach the jungle floor. They suggest Westwood hover as close to treetop level as possible."

"For crissake, Sparkman! We were going to do that anyway. What's the name of the man in the hoist?"

"Lancaster, sir," Sparkman said. "George F."

"Give me the command net."

Sparkman flipped a phone off his shoulder, caught it, and thrust the phone into the OD's hand.

"Okay, shooters," asked Daniels, "did you find that landing zone for me?"

"The double ridges," answered the first Cobra pilot. "It's also where Charlie fired at us."

"But too far away," said the second pilot.

The OD looked at the map and agreed.

"Easy to see why they chose that spot," continued the pilot. "It's the only place they could get a clear shot at Falcon's chopper."

"Anything else?" Daniels demanded, gripping the phone so tight his knuckles were turning white. "Anything relevant?"

"Magic Mountain," offered the other pilot.

At the front of the room, Daniels watched the skinny

major move his metal pointer between the crash site and Magic Mountain, a terrain feature located farther inside Cambodia, then move the pointer between the presumed crash site and the Cambodian border. All three locations were on a line running east and west and appeared to be connected by a trail. At least, from this side of the border, a trail disappeared into the jungle, and there were reports that the Ho Chi Minh Trail ran through the NVA base camp, continued past Magic Mountain, and meandered into South Vietnam.

"Magic Mountain's too far away," Daniels said. "We might as well walk in from this side."

"Forward observers on station in fifteen minutes," reported a voice that Daniels barely heard.

"Lurp team!" shouted Manley from Cromley's desk. "The Blue Jay Team!"

All heads turned in his direction, and Sparkman flipped a dial and held up a different phone. "They're on here, sir."

Daniels snatched the phone out of Sparkman's hand, and the RTO had to be quick to catch the command net phone before it landed in his lap.

Finally some good news, thought Daniels. There might be only six of them, operating deep in enemy territory and without fire support, but a good recon team could spirit Falcon away from danger. Hell, when a live prisoner was needed for interrogation, it was the long-range recon teams that were sent in to capture one of the bastards.

"Where are you, Blue Jay?"

"About a klick due west of my night site." The voice

on the radiotelephone had a Southern accent as it read off some letters of the alphabet. "We're en route to the crash site. Can you give me those numbers?"

As Daniels read the letters off the blackboard beside the map of South Vietnam, Blue Jay's ambush site for that night was fed into the computer. The OD tapped his fingers on the console while the information was decoded. On all other lines you could talk as you pleased—they were secured—but no one had invented a scrambler light enough to be carried by a small unit commander. Until then all locations were encoded in case Charlie was listening and wanted to drop a few rounds on your position.

The computer flashed the translated numbers on its screen, but before the soldier operating the IBM could call out Blue Jay's coordinates, the skinny major read the numbers over the man's shoulder and slapped his metal pointer against the map.

Anticipation drained out of everyone, especially the officer of the day. The long-range reconnaissance team was too far away. The airborne company would arrive sooner. All Blue Jay was good for was backup, and did he really want to send a lurp team into the jaws of an NVA recon in force, one that for sure had to be moving toward the crash site?

"Keep moving, Blue Jay," advised Daniels, "and keep us posted as to your position."

"Wilco. Out."

Daniels gripped the console. It was time to send down the man in the hoist; the only chance to fix Falcon's location, but not much of a chance for the man in the hoist. With the CIC's chopper down in enemy territory, what other choice did they have? The OD leaned into the console and stared at the huge operational map. Flanking it were maps displaying the location of both friendly and enemy dispositions.

Where are you, Falcon? How far did you fall? Did you get lucky and end up in the tangles or did you hit bottom, making it irrelevant who reaches you first?

Daniels straightened up and spoke into a phone Sparkman had somehow slipped into his hand. "Go, Lancaster! Go!"

CHAPTER
FIVE

Sergeant George Francis Lancaster checked the harness running over his shoulders, around his waist, and under his crotch. He felt behind his back for the machete and beside his belt for the pistol and canteen. Under his arms were extra smoke canisters about the size of soft-drink cans, and on his back, a radio. Strapped across his chest was a knife, handle down and blade up—handle wrapped with thin strands of leather so that it would not slip out of a sweaty or bloody hand—and in one of the large pockets of his jungle fatigues, a flashlight. He had been told he'd need that on the jungle floor. Lancaster held onto the wire that would lower him into the jungle, leaned out, and surveyed the unbroken sea of green.

How'd they expect him to find anything down there, and since he wouldn't be able to, why drop him into that green at all? Didn't they know he had less than two weeks left in this miserable little country? All he wanted was to go home to Judy and the boys. He'd even take that job working for his father-in-law. It wasn't fair. Not fair at all. Only a few weeks ago, his first sergeant had given him the good news.

"By all rights you should be dead, Lancaster. Charlie whacked your squad but good."

Lancaster had stood at ease in front of a couple of wooden ammo boxes that served as the first sergeant's desk. He knew better than to interrupt when the first sergeant was preaching.

"When the relief column arrived you were the only one alive. That's the second time that's happened to you, boy, and both times you've come out without a scratch. You're overdue. It's best you don't go back into the field. But everyone has to put in their twelve months, so I scrounged up this job where all you have to do is sit on your butt and ride shotgun. It's called 'Heroes Patrol.' So get out of here and see if you can stay out of trouble for the next four weeks."

Lancaster hung onto the wire, scanned the green sea below, and shook his head. *I did what you told me, First Sergeant. I tried to stay out of trouble, but somewhere along the line something messed up and they're about to drop me into a jungle full of Charlies. First Sergeant, I do believe I wasn't meant to get out of this miserable little country alive.*

"Go, Lancaster! Go!" came the word through his headset, and Lancaster knew the order had been given by some guy in an air-conditioned bunker back in Long Bien.

Lancaster held on tight to the overhead wire and

stepped into the air. Using his free hand, he pushed away from the Huey that hovered at treetop level, its skids touching the topmost branches. As he was lowered away, he spun around until the wire stabilized. Lancaster didn't like this one bit. Not one little bit.

The Huey dropped him under the branches of a large cauliflower-shaped tree, and then through an open space, before the foliage became thicker. The next layer was coming up fast and looked like a bunch of upside-down mops.

"Lancaster, how much room do you have?" asked the sissy pants back in Long Bien.

What was the guy talking about? Didn't the man know he was hanging on a wire out here? "What you mean, Eagle's Nest?"

"I mean, if Westwood wanted to move you to all four points of the compass, could he?"

Lancaster looked around and understood why the compass had been strapped to his wrist. "Can't move to the south. There's a tree behind me. East and west are crowded; north is wide open."

"That's how it's done," said the voice from Long Bien. "Now don't forget. It'll come in handy farther down."

Something flew overhead and Lancaster ducked. "Dad-burn! What was that?"

"What was what?" The voice from Long Bien was tense. Anxious.

"A cat flew by, and I mean a cat, too, sir. Not some squirrel. Holy moley, would you look at her go? I'll bet she covered a hundred feet or more and with one jump. Landed on a tree, and she looks no worse for the wear."

Lancaster forgot the line was paying out and sat down on top of one of the mop-like trees. "Stop! Stop!"

The wire jerked, biting into his crotch. Dad-gummit! He and Judy had planned on having a little girl when he got home. He'd have to pay more attention to what he was doing.

He glanced at his compass. "Take me up two to three yards, then two or three more yards to . . . the north."

Westwood complied, and after finishing the maneuver began lowering Lancaster again. The man on the wire wasn't the least surprised. He was being sent in not to kill Charlies but to kill the suspense back in Long Bien.

As Lancaster moved through the second layer of the triple canopy, the real enemy began to show itself. Lancaster slapped at a bug taking a bite out of him, and looking up, he saw Westwood disappear overhead. The jungle became darker, cooler, and more alive. A parrot climbed a tree using its beak as a third foot. Some kind of see-through frog leaped across his path, multicolored butterflies fluttered by, and cicadas (he figured they were cicadas) cranked up a song.

The jungle was coming up thick and fast now, giving him just enough time to dodge branches and slip through the vines. The appearance of the vines was something new. They hadn't been in the layer he'd just come through. Lancaster pushed several away . . . and one turned out to be a snake. He jerked back, let go, and watched the snake fall away, disappearing in the darkness below.

"Good-bye, you son of a gun." Then to Westwood:

"Okay, go left." Lancaster glanced at the compass. "I mean east . . . five yards. Yeah, that's it, but you're dropping me too fast. Westwood, you've got to slow down. It's getting pretty thick down here . . . dad-blamed tree!

"Oh," groaned Lancaster. "Dad-gummit, you didn't have to stop. Okay, we're around the tree. Ten to fifteen feet to the south it clears out for a while. Steady. Steady. Steady as she goes."

Birds chirped, frogs croaked, and cicadas continued to sing away as the jungle grew thicker. Around Lancaster the canopy became a jumble of branches interlaced with vines, and the vines were everywhere, some thicker than a man's arm. The vines hadn't been satisfied to merely crawl into a tree; but once they were topside, they'd crossed into the tree's neighbor and its neighbor's neighbor, leaving little room to maneuver.

"Hold up!"

The wire jerked to a stop and Lancaster moaned again. He stared at the layer below him. How the devil was he supposed to get through all that? He looked left and right for some kind of passage, any kind of way through all this . . . this green-and-brown spaghetti. It couldn't be this thick everywhere. He asked Westwood to lift him up for a look-see, but the tangles didn't look any more passable from twenty feet higher.

The voice in Long Bien asked, "Why aren't you moving?"

"This place is thick with vines. And there's no sign of Falcon's chopper."

"Doubt you'll see it until you're on the ground."

"Anything on the old command net?"

"No."

Lancaster was stalling and the sissy pants knew it. But no one told him he'd have to plow through all these tangles. Charlie would hear him coming, and from the ground, this ole boy would be easy pickings.

Lancaster fingered the pistol at his side. "How you gonna get me out of here?"

"Pull you through the hole cut by the chopper. Just because you can't see it doesn't mean it's not there."

Oh, yeah? Then why don't you come out here and take a look. "So I have to find Falcon's chopper to get out of here?"

"That's the drill. Now get moving, Lancaster, and don't fight the vines. That'll only wear you out. Weave around them. It'll be much easier once you're on the jungle floor. Nothing grows down there. Not enough light." The voice paused. "By the way, you may not have enough line to reach the ground."

Though Lancaster had worked up a sweat coming down, he chilled at this new piece of information. "I'm going to have to let go of the line?" Suddenly the aggravation across his back that ran under his crotch became very dear to him.

"You'd have to anyway. There's no way you could move around with that line on your back."

Now why hadn't he thought of that?

Because he'd always figured if he got into any trouble, all Westwood would have to do was jerk him to safety.

Lancaster looked up. The overhead was thick with trees, limbs, and vines. Westwood would pound him to death saving his life.

Canada. He should've run off to Canada with Bennie James. James had run for it, why hadn't he? Because of a sense of loyalty to what? A country about to get him killed—for the third time. If he'd run off, he never would've had to go through all this. Or end up working for Judy's father.

Judy. That's why he hadn't run off—he didn't want her thinking he was a coward—and now the dad-blamed army was making sure he'd never see her again. Bennie James would return home after this war was over and claim her. It wasn't fair, not fair at all, but he did hope Bennie would be a good father to his boys. What Bennie might tell his sons about their daddy's service record, Lancaster didn't even want to think about.

Long Bien ordered him lowered away, and Lancaster turned up his collar and waded into the tangles. He turned up his collar because of the ants. From other missions he knew the little devils could eat you alive. Lancaster slipped, slid, and fell through the tangles, the vines catching his arms, hooking his feet, and slapping him across the face. Every time he hit a vine or branch, more of the little red monsters were dumped on top of him.

The ants were everywhere, crawling across his arms, down his neck, and inside his shirt. Taking time to brush them away only gave the little devils more time to hitch a ride. Many did not venture far from where they landed, but bit into him as soon as they came aboard. Lancaster finally gave up and concentrated on pushing through this final layer as fast as possible.

Feast, you little bastards, because when I'm on the ground, I'm going to strip off this dad-gum shirt and squash every darn one of you. Squash you flat, that's what I'm going to do. That is, if I don't have to hide in this thicket from Charlie. Lancaster didn't want to think about hiding in these tangles while the ants went about the work of stripping the meat off his bones.

He stopped and looked around. Darn! Everything looked the same—to the left, the right, above and below. Even where he'd just come through had already closed up behind him. If it wasn't for gravity, he'd never know which way was up—or down—and would spend the rest of his life fumbling around in this layer of the jungle canopy. He slapped at an ant. That is, until the ants finished eating him alive.

A lizard leaped across his path and Lancaster backed away, bumping into a limb and showering himself with even more ants. He tried to brush them off, but there were just too many, and places on his shirt turned red as their army marched across his chest. The ants were everywhere, even making their way up under his fatigue cap. He was being scalped alive!

To heck with this!

Lancaster reached over his shoulder to pull out his machete, accidentally freeing the radio's previously lashed-down antenna, which added to his problems of moving through the tangles. Vines and branches fell across his path as he hacked his way through. Forgotten was any thought of the enemy hearing him coming. All he wanted was out of here—away from these little monsters and their dad-gum teeth!

FALLEN STARS

He crashed forward, slicing through anything and everything in his path, avoiding trees and larger limbs, but only after a solid whack told him couldn't pass that way. In minutes, his arms ached, then went numb, but still Lancaster slashed on, watching the work of a right arm seemingly no longer attached to his body. Sweat ran down his face and his fatigues became soaked. But he wasn't going to stop. He wouldn't stop! He was getting out of here! Getting away from these little red monsters! He was going to break through if it was the last thing—

Lancaster popped out of the tangles and came face to face with a long-limbed, orange creature. He dropped the machete, leaped back into the thicket, and fumbled around for his pistol. When he looked again, the orangutan swung under the limb it had been sitting on. Upside down the creature stared up at him, and Lancaster stared back. The orangutan hung from the very limb Lancaster needed to use to reach the ground, which was right below him, less than thirty feet away.

He'd made it! And still no sign of Charlie. Now if that dad-gum monkey would only get out of his way. The blasted thing hung from the only vine that gave him access to the ground. Lancaster waved his hands, dousing himself with more ants.

"Shoo! You get out of here!"

But the upside-down, reddish-brown creature only stared at him. And wouldn't you know it, the voice in Long Bien chose that moment to ask for a report.

"Give me a sit rep."

Jiminy Cricket! What do I tell him—that I've been

stopped by a monkey? "Sir, I can see the ground, but it's pretty dark down there. Maybe I oughta take it slow until my eyes adjust to the darkness." Forgotten were the ants stripping the flesh from his bones.

"Get down there, soldier! You're playing with men's lives!"

Yeah, but there's only one life you're worried about and it sure ain't mine. Lancaster moved in the direction of the orangutan and found he needed more line.

"You've got it all," Westwood said.

Darn. No slack. The story of his life.

The orangutan blinked, then moved hand over hand and foot over foot to a tree where it shimmied to the ground. Without looking back, the animal wandered off into the darkness.

"Thank you," said Lancaster, putting away his pistol.

Slapping at the ants, he surveyed the darkness. Except for some light flecks, the jungle floor was empty, just like they'd told him. Guess there was no reason not to go down there.

Lancaster sighed, unbuckled the harness, and turned it loose. He was lowering the radio to the ground by a piece of nylon rope when he heard an unjungle-like noise.

Someone crying!

Someone from the chopper?

In his haste to reach the ground, Lancaster grabbed the limb the orangutan had used and swung out on it. The limb snapped under his weight and his feet flew out in front of him. He landed on his back on the jungle floor, the breath knocked out of him. As he lay there, trying to catch his breath, brightly colored lights flashed, except at the corners of his eyes. At the corners, his vision had gone dark.

In a few moments he sat up, moved his arms and legs, and ran a hand up his back. No broken bones. He'd been lucky. Lucky as hell. He could've landed on a stump or log, even the radio. Might've broken his darn neck. *Dad-blast it. Make it all the way down here, and then get clobbered by a stump. Yeah. That'd figure.*

Lancaster looked around, and as he did, felt the mushy bottom of the jungle floor. On second thought maybe he couldn't have landed on anything. There was nothing here but trees with trunks as thick as barrels, and vines growing into the first layer of the jungle canopy. The air seemed cooler but felt thicker.

Lancaster listened but heard nothing. No one crying. Matter of fact, the jungle was dead quiet. That in itself was eerie, but a terrific opportunity to rid himself of all these dad-blamed ants. Lancaster stripped off his equipment and shirt and shook out every last one of the little devils. And those that wouldn't take the hint, he smushed. Whew! Finally some relief. Except for the itching. He'd have to put up with that until he located the chopper. They'd have a first-aid kit aboard. Jiminy! It was hard to remember why he'd been sent down here in the first place; that's how distracting the jungle was.

Lancaster pulled on his shirt and shouldered his way into his equipment. He was slapping ants out of his hat when he thought he heard the sound of crying again. A woman crying. Lancaster stopped and listened.

Yes. A woman was crying out here in the middle of the jungle. Maybe one of Charlie's wives? Maybe the chopper had landed on her husband, killing him, and the woman was all broke up?

Or could it be the reporter who had gone up with Falcon today?

"Yo!"

"What!" came the sound of a woman's voice out of the darkness and to his right. "Is there someone there?"

"Keep talking." Lancaster moved in her direction, taking along the radio and the equipment on his web belt.

"Are you really there?" asked the woman. "But how . . . ?"

"Don't stop talking. I can't find you if you stop talking." Lancaster pointed the light in the direction of the woman's voice.

"Oh, thank God, you found me! We're right over here. I can see your light. Who are you?"

"Sergeant George F. Lancaster. I was in the trail Huey. Keep talking. I can hear you, but can't see you, or the chopper." Lancaster moved faster, weaving his way around the vines and the barrel-sized trees.

"I can't believe you found us. Did you run into Rodriguez? Rodriguez told me to stay put. Not to move. He had a funny look in his eyes. I think he was hurt and didn't know it."

Lancaster stumbled over a log, and the log moaned. Rodriguez. Lancaster knelt down, felt the copilot's neck, and found a pulse. He was alive! But what about Falcon? He started in the direction of the chopper again. "How's Falcon?"

The woman didn't answer.

"The general. Is he okay?"

Still no answer.

"Hey, lady, can you still hear me?"

"He's . . . dead."

Lancaster's heart sank. Sweet Jesus. How would he tell Long Bien? Lancaster gripped the web belt holding the radio. Bad news could always wait. "Uh—keep talking. Anyone else alive?"

"No, but I'm right here. Can you see me? I'm waiting for you, Sergeant Lancaster. Didn't you say that was your name? I stayed in the helicopter like Rodriguez told me. Did I do right?"

Now he could see the chopper and it was a mess. No wonder Falcon was dead. The Huey had slammed into a tree—a big one, too—and had slid down to the base. The tail was entangled in the same vines Lancaster had fought his way through and the Plexiglas nose was smashed. Rammed through the glass was a limb, and two of the helicopter's blades were bent straight up, one even snapped off.

"Yeah, you did the right thing."

The woman had her helmet off but remained in the web seat. A long crack ran down the back of the helmet held in her lap. If she hadn't had that helmet on, her brains would've been pouring out of her head instead of her long blond hair. The woman fumbled with her seat belt but was unable to pop it loose. Not a mark on the girl, but the pilot in the seat ahead of her, his head was twisted at a funny angle.

Falcon lay face down in the open cabin, blood oozing from his head. As Lancaster closed with the chopper, he further surveyed his surroundings. The general's aide and the other reporter were nowhere to be seen.

"He was in the chair beside me," said the woman. "The belt didn't hold." She held up the broken strap and glanced at the body on the deck. "He—he saved my life." Tears started down her cheeks.

"It's okay, lady. Everything's going to be all right."

Which was nothing more than a big fat lie. Somebody would be held accountable, and along the way, the dad-blame army would find some way to extend his stay in this miserable little country.

Lancaster dropped the radio to the ground and grasped one of the helicopter's skids that hung five or six feet off the jungle floor. Gripping the metal tubing of the harness chair, he pulled himself into the cabin. A voice from the front of the chopper caused him to jump.

"How you doing, Lancaster?" It was the pilot, pinned to his seat by the limb through the Plexiglas shield. The pilot looked at him out of the corner of his eye.

"Er—good, sir. Let me get you out of there."

"No! Don't touch me! I can't feel a thing. Can't move my arms or legs. Leave me for the medics."

"I thought you were dead."

"Probably am, just don't know it yet. Sorry to give you such a start, but I come and go, and whenever I've regained consciousness, the damn woman's been crying for her daddy. Thought it best to keep my mouth shut."

Lancaster stared at the woman, who hung her head. Evidently in shock. Probably what happens when the chopper you're riding in falls out of the sky. You want your mommy. Or your daddy. Lancaster didn't want to know. Coming down on a hoist had been thrill enough, thank you very much.

"Have you checked the status of the CIC?"

"The lady said he was dead."

"She's been in that seat ever since we landed. Get down on your hands and knees, Sergeant, and see if you can find a pulse."

Lancaster did as ordered, touching Falcon's neck, and found a pulse. "Sweet Jesus! He's alive. I can't believe it. He's alive!"

"Never take the word of a civilian."

The woman fought with her belt, and when it wouldn't release, she reached over and jerked down on the handle of the knife, releasing the weapon from its sheath strapped across Lancaster's chest. She sliced the belt in half and slid to the floor beside Falcon. Lancaster never saw her. He was too excited.

He'd done it! Not only had he located the chopper but found the CO. Alive. Alive, dad-gummit! He was going to get out of this miserable little country after all. Out of the corner of his eye he saw the pilot pinned to his seat. Lancaster flushed with shame. For the pilot there would be no such celebration. But he could get the man out of here and on his way home.

"Got a radio?" asked the pilot.

"Yes, sir."

"Good, 'cause mine's kinda on the blink."

Glancing at the control panel, Lancaster saw the radio had been knocked out of the board by the same limb pinning the pilot to his seat. That's why Rodriguez had set out on foot and left the woman in her seat. The jungle was no place for a woman.

"Then get on with it, Sergeant. That is, if you have some plan how to get us out of here."

"As soon as Long Bien knows our location, they're going to hook you out of here with a McGuire Rig."

"Well, I don't know how this old bod's going to react to being jerked out of the jungle on some rope and harness, but I do want out of this damn jungle."

Lancaster dropped from the cabin to the ground. As he ran for the radio, his feet hardly touched the ground. This was one call he wouldn't mind making, but first he had to pop smoke. Green smoke. That's what they had agreed on. If he found the chopper, pop green smoke, one hell of a lot green smoke. If he ran into Charlie, red smoke.

"Where are you going?"

The woman was trying to fit one of her boots on the skid so she could follow him to the ground.

Lancaster unhooked a canister from the web belt. "I have to get a hoist in here."

Hanging on the helicopter, one foot on the skid, one foot off, the woman stared beyond him.

Lancaster looked behind him. There were only a handful of them, but all of them wore black pajamas and carried Russian-made assault rifles. Lancaster knew he should pop red smoke, lots of red smoke, but he didn't think Charlie would give him the chance.

CHAPTER
SIX

"They have found the helicopter!" shouted the North Vietnamese major assigned to monitor the frequency of the Viet Cong squad on the east-west trail.

Everyone left the map and hurried over to the communications table. Gzap snubbed out another cigarette, put on the headset, and picked up the microphone. Now what was said could be heard only by him, and that was just the way Gzap wanted it.

"Tell me what you have found."

"An American Huey, sir!" shouted the squad leader, his voice crackling with excitement. He went on to describe the damage to the downed helicopter.

Gzap fought to control his own excitement. If this was true, this would get Hanoi off his back for months. "Passengers?"

"Five, sir. One of them a woman."

"The Americans have a woman with them?"

Gzap's staff stared at their leader in disbelief. The Americans were notorious for failing to fully utilize half of their able-bodied population. The NVA could not afford to be so choosy. They had been fighting this war for more than twenty years, and alongside them, their women.

"Yes, sir. A woman."

"Why is she there?"

"I—I have no idea. None of the prisoners speak our language."

Gzap cursed his enemies for not learning the local language. "Try French." A minute later he received a negative report regarding that, too. He turned to the lieutenant from Hanoi. "Do you speak English, boy?"

The young man flushed and shook his head.

To his first sergeant, Gzap said, "Bien speaks some English but has already left, is that correct?"

"Yes, sir. Quite a few minutes ago."

"Then find Sergeant Dung and bring him here. And prepare another platoon to move out for the east-west trail. I will not lose those prisoners."

"Yes, sir."

As the first sergeant hurried out of the command hut, Gzap returned his attention to the crash site. The Americans were sure to make some kind of rescue attempt, and when that attempt came, he planned to have the prisoners as far away from the crash site as possible.

To the squad leader on the east-west trail he said, "Sergeant, have your second in command ready the prisoners to move out. As he is doing this, give me the rank and physical condition of each prisoner, including the woman. I want to know what you have."

At the crash site, the squad leader ordered someone to organize a detail to return the unconscious Rodriguez to the helicopter. Then, starting with Lancaster, the squad leader read off the American's rank, recognizing his opposite number's insignia.

"There is little wrong with him, sir, but for a good number of bug bites."

"I just want to know if they can walk!" snapped Gzap. "Or will they have to be carried out?"

"Yes, sir!" The squad leader said the woman could walk, identified her as "press" but did not know what that meant.

Gzap did and the news excited him. Reporters usually traveled with colonels or higher. Perhaps he had caught a big fish after all. "And her name?"

"Casey Blackburn," said the squad leader, having difficulty with the pronunciation. "She introduced herself to me."

When Gzap repeated the information for his aide, the young lieutenant from Hanoi burst out, "Casey Blackburn! I know her! She is a friend of the Party. I met her when she interviewed Uncle Ho."

Gzap stared at the young man. He doubted any American was a friend of the Party, but if those fools in Hanoi thought so, who was he to disagree?

"What else do you have?" asked Gzap.

The squad leader climbed into the open bay of the downed helicopter, the radio on his back making it tough duty. Two of his men gave him a boost and he finished his climb into the bay, where he was able to identify the pilot as a warrant officer. He said it appeared the man's neck was broken.

"If that was so," Gzap said, "he would be dead."

"Yes—yes, sir."

While the Viet Cong were busy with the downed aircraft and its prisoners, Lancaster drifted backwards. Four Viet Cong surrounded the unconscious Rodriguez, trying to figure out how to pick up someone as heavy as an American and keep their rifles at the ready. They finally decided to tie the prisoner's hands behind his back. Then they shouldered their rifles and picked him up.

Seeing no one was watching him, Lancaster went to one knee, snatched up the web belt with the radio, and backed away toward the dusk that was clinging to the jungle floor. The radio was on, the mike in his hand. All he needed was a few seconds—

Something jabbed him in the back!

Lancaster turned around, ever so slowly, still gripping the radio. He released the push-to-talk button. A Viet Cong stood behind him. Using his rifle, the Viet Cong gestured Lancaster back to the helicopter. The darkness of the jungle floor cut both ways. Hidden from sight had been a picket line of security surrounding the downed chopper.

Lancaster was returning to the helicopter and tapping out an SOS with the mike when he was jabbed in the back again. He turned around and saw the Vietnamese motioning for him to drop the radio. Lancaster frowned, finished a few more clicks on the mike, and then dropped the radio before returning to the chopper. As he did, he said a quick prayer for an early arrival of the unit that had to be in the air and on their way here. But they'd better find a faster way to penetrate the jungle roof or it'd take hours for them to locate Falcon's position.

Inside the Huey, the squad leader was having a difficult time identifying the American lying unconscious on the floor of the open bay. He had never paid much attention to any American above the rank of captain, assuming he would never run into anyone of such stature. He had no idea what the four black stars sewn into the collar of the unconscious man's military blouse meant. The man might be some kind of general, but, really, what were his chances of capturing a general, especially one wearing four stars? In the North Vietnamese Army, there were fewer than two or three generals of equivalent rank.

On the other end of the line, Gzap could not believe what he was hearing. Evidently the squad leader was a complete fool. "Would you describe the insignia again?"

The man did and Gzap was stunned. His ancestors did approve of which side of the war he had taken. Capturing an American general could make a general out of him. Four stars . . . there could be only one . . . could it be—no, that was impossible. Probably a visitor from Washington trying to earn some silly combat ribbon the Americans gave to those who flew over a combat zone.

"And his name?"

This pressed the squad leader beyond his ability, so the Vietnamese asked Lancaster, who had returned to the helicopter.

Lancaster played dumb.

Casey Blackburn watched all this with growing fascination. The VC tugged on the general's name tag and shouted at the American but Lancaster stood mute.

Why not say the man's name? The general was already a prisoner, and there was nothing Lancaster could do about it. Hell, Casey would even tell the VC, but she was here to report the news, not make it.

The squad leader spoke sharply to the men beside her. A soldier grabbed Casey from behind, holding her where she stood. Another put a rifle to her head. Casey gasped and tried to back away but was held in place. The cool metal of the barrel pressed against her temple. She tried to speak but found her voice gone. She looked at Lancaster, eyes pleading. Lancaster looked at the ground and spit out the name. The squad leader repeated the name to Gzap.

The colonel could not believe what he had heard. He asked the squad leader to repeat the name.

"I am sorry, sir, but American names . . . they are beyond me."

"Would you stop apologizing and simply repeat the name?"

The squad leader did, and Gzap asked for a chair. The RTO leaped out of his chair and slid it under the colonel as he collapsed into it. Everyone in the hut stared at their glassy-eyed leader. No one had ever seen Gzap like this before. Had the helicopter exploded? Had all their men been killed? Had an American rescue team arrived, using some fantastic technology to rescue their people?

Gzap looked up and told his staff who their prisoner was. The command hut went absolutely silent, then exploded in a roar that caused the first sergeant to hurry inside, another sergeant right on his heels. When told the news, they, too, joined in the celebration.

But at the crash site, the silence on the net made the squad leader nervous. He called the base camp repeatedly but received no answer. All transmissions from there had ceased. Why now, of all times?

The squad leader pulled off the radio and shook it. He was fiddling with the dials when his men brought the unconscious Rodriguez over. The squad leader leaped to the ground and passed on the information about the unconscious warrant officer to the base camp.

Still no reply.

The squad leader snapped at his men, and Lancaster and Blackburn's hands were quickly tied behind their backs. A broken radio would be no defense for the loss of any prisoners. When Gzap finally returned to the air, the squad leader could barely hear him. It sounded as if there was a party going on at the base camp.

"Can the general walk?" asked Gzap, raising his voice over the celebration.

"He is unconscious, sir." The squad leader gaped at the man lying on the flight deck, realization sinking in. He scanned the dusk of the jungle floor; then after a glance at the overhead canopy, he ordered his squad in a tight perimeter around the chopper.

"Are you still there?" demanded Gzap.

"Just double-checking my security."

"Good. I want the general moved to the east-west

trail and I want him moved there fast. Use a stretcher if one is available, or carry him, but move him out of there. As for you, upon your return to our base camp, you will receive a chest full of medals and a trip to Hanoi to honor your effort."

The squad leader didn't have to be told what would happen if he failed to return with the general. "Do I make stretchers for all the wounded?"

"No time for that. The Americans could be there at any moment. Now listen and listen carefully." And Gzap gave the squad leader his instructions. He finished with, "Lieutenant Bien will rendezvous with you at the base of Magic Mountain."

The squad leader was not pleased with this last piece of information. No one liked Lieutenant Bien. Bien was the type of soldier who would try to take credit for capturing the American general himself.

"Keep the general and the radio with you at all times. By the time you return everyone will know the name of the newest hero in our struggle to reunite our country."

✳   ✳   ✳

In the Long Bien bunker, RTO Sparkman looked up from his radio. "Sir, it's been over twenty minutes since Lancaster's last report."

"Call him again," said Daniels, wandering over to the communications console.

"I just did, sir, but I can't raise him. Just some Morse code clicks."

"Saying what?"

"SOS."

"But not identifying the sender?"

"That is correct, sir."

"Then it could be anyone." Hopefully, Falcon, thought Daniels, and not some fool playing on the command net. "Keep trying. And keep listening."

"Yes, sir."

Daniels stared at the clock over the map. The local time was flanked by clocks showing the time in Washington, Clark Air Force Base in the Philippines, Honolulu, and San Francisco. Daylight was fading fast. Where the hell was Lancaster? The whole operation would run much smoother with a man on the ground, especially one with a radio.

Daniels sighed. The man in the hoist had been one option. Now they'd move onto the next option, a plan that involved more men and machinery and was much more dependable. Sending a man down in a hoist had been forced on them by circumstances, but in a war zone a single soldier didn't make that much difference.

"Manley," Daniels asked the captain subbing at the airborne desk, "where are your men?"

"In the air, sir, crossing the border. ETA to the crash site less than ten minutes."

Daniels nodded. In fifteen minutes he would have a complete company of those men on the ground. He looked at the air force liaison, who answered Daniels' question before he could ask it.

"The plane with the infrared photos is on the ground. The pictures were developed during the return flight."

"Make sure that airborne unit has that location,"

Daniels said to Manley. Through a phone handed to him by Sparkman, he asked the pilot hovering over the crash site, "How much fuel remaining, Westwood?"

"Twenty minutes."

"Roger. When your replacements arrive, you're free to return home. Fire Support Base Tango is expecting you to refuel there."

"What about the man in the hoist?"

"He fell on his head or something. When you leave, cut the line."

A tremor ran through every man in the command center. No one left Americans behind, no matter how hot the terrain, and everyone in the command center had requested a buddy make sure his body was returned to the States; some of the men in this room had already had to honor such a request.

"Your replacements will find him," added Daniels when he saw everyone staring at him.

"Er—roger," said Westwood. "When the airborne unit arrives, I'll cut the line to the man on the ground and return to Fire Support Base Tango, where I'll refuel before returning to your location. Westwood out."

CHAPTER SEVEN

The Viet Cong moved their prisoners from the crash site to the east-west trail, which ran from the base of Magic Mountain to the Cambodian/Vietnamese border. Since Falcon was still groggy and unable to walk, the VC carried him on a stretcher taken from the Huey, hands tied behind his back. The squad leader was taking no chances. There was more than this general's life at stake.

As Casey Blackburn stumbled along in the growing darkness, she realized there would be no daddy coming to her rescue, maybe no one at all. Out here she was on her own. But if she kept her wits about her, she might come out of this alive and with a hell of a story. Still, on this trail, in the middle of this jungle, with rifles being swung around nervously, until she found someone who appreciated her work she'd best stay on her toes. Those rifles could kill a journalist as easy as any GI.

The Viet Cong with the radio strapped to his back fired his rifle into the air several times, then walked over and thrust the radio handset to her ear. Already wincing from the rifle shots, Casey backed away. The Vietnamese grabbed her arm, forcing her ear against the handset that was protected by a plastic bag. Over the man's shoulder the whip antenna danced in the twilight of the jungle floor.

"Miss Blackburn, can you hear me?" asked a voice in heavily accented English.

"Er—yes. Yes, I can." Casey cleared her throat and leaned her ear against the handset, forcing the plastic down so that she could make out what was being said.

"I am Sergeant Dung. I am in the battalion base camp where our men will be bringing you." Dung asked Casey to reconfirm who the captured general was, and after she had, the Vietnamese said, "We have hospitals. The general will receive medical attention. I understand he was injured in the crash."

"Knocked out."

Casey had to explain what "knocked out" meant. Once she had, Dung said, "Very well, Miss Blackburn. The general will be well treated here, as all American prisoners are. Would you be the same Casey Blackburn who interviewed our beloved Party leader in Hanoi?"

"I am." That interview had really made her father flip out, and Casey had received one of his infrequent letters, a tirade running the gamut from consorting with the enemy to embarrassing him among his peers.

"You have a reputation for fairness, Miss Blackburn."

"Thank you." Well, if she had any kind of reputation

now was the time to find out how well it was received. "I can understand why the sergeant's hands are tied but not mine or the general's. The general's unconscious and I'm a member of the press. I want our hands untied." She flashed a warm smile at the Viet Cong wearing the radio and moved away, strolling down the trail in the direction of Falcon's stretcher.

The squad leader put the handset to his ear expecting to hear further instructions from Dung. Instead he heard a string of brusque questions. The squad leader tried to explain what the woman had done, even going so far as to point at where she stood, which Sergeant Dung could not possibly see. After getting an earful, the squad leader followed Casey down the trail and tried to put the handset to her ear again. She dodged away, smiling and shaking her head.

The squad leader was confused. This woman was one of the prisoners he was responsible for, but she was also interfering with the performance of the mission. Colonel Gzap had told him he could shoot anyone who interfered with the completion of this mission. The squad leader spoke quickly into the headset, nodded at the answer, and shouted at one of his men. A Viet Cong pulled a knife and advanced upon the woman.

Casey stepped back. Maybe she'd overestimated her importance. Maybe she was just pissing in the wind, as her father so eloquently described her line of work.

The VC grabbed Casey's arm, whirled her around and sliced through the rope. The blade scraped her wrist as it went through. Falcon, however, was left tied up with several Vietnamese guarding his stretcher. A bandage covered the general's head. He moaned but made no move to sit up.

The squad leader returned to Casey, who was massaging her wrists. She took the handset to speak with Dung again. "Yes?"

"That is all I can do. As inhumane as it may seem, tying the general's hands is the best way to keep him alive. The general will certainly try to escape, as I would if I were in the same situation. And warn your Sergeant Lancaster not to attempt to escape. Our soldiers have orders to kill him, as they do you."

She relayed to Lancaster what Dung had said.

"They're playing you for a sucker, lady."

Casey shook her head. Lancaster didn't understand. He didn't have to file a story when they reached Hanoi. She returned to the radio and Dung taught her how to ask for the handset in Vietnamese.

"We do not want any misunderstandings, Miss Blackburn, but we will do our duty."

While Casey was practicing how to ask for the radio, shots rang out from the crash site. Startled, she looked in that direction.

"The bastards," muttered Lancaster.

"What was that?" Casey asked the squad leader.

The VC only pointed at the handset.

"Sergeant Dung," she asked, "there were shots from the crash site. What's happening?"

"Soldiers are moving in your direction. The ones you are with are signaling their position."

Remembering the firing that had caused her to wince,

Casey said, "The squad leader has already done that."

"Then I can only assume one of the pilots tried to escape."

Casey told Lancaster what Dung had said.

"Is that so?" asked Lancaster, his voice dripping with sarcasm. "Then ask your friend which one: the unconscious one or the one with the broken back?"

Casey felt as if she'd been hit in the chest. She couldn't breathe. She looked down the trail. Neither pilot was there, only Falcon. The pilots had remained at the crash site.

"You bastards!" she screamed into the handset. "You lied to me! You killed the pilots because they couldn't walk, and you'd do the same to me. All you want is the damn general!" And Casey jerked down, snapping the wire connecting the handset to the radio.

The motion caused the squad leader to be pulled toward her. After righting himself, he stared at the broken cord and the handset in the plastic sack. His mouth fell open as the woman sneered at him and tossed the handset off into the darkness of the jungle floor.

The squad leader couldn't believe what he had just seen. The penalty for a lost or damaged radio was death. He stared into the darkness of the jungle floor. Locating the handset was of little importance. All that mattered was a radio had been damaged, and that he had allowed this woman to do it. He was a dead man. But before they killed him, he would kill the woman. His orders gave him that right. The squad leader whipped around, and in the same motion, slapped her across the face.

The blow snapped Casey's head to one side, and she stumbled backwards, too startled to defend herself. As abusive as her father had been, he had never struck her. No one had ever struck her. Before Casey could bring her hands up to defend herself, the squad leader slapped her again, again, and again.

Stars flew; Casey's face stung, then went numb, and her legs weakened. She sat down hard. Through flashing lights, she saw a blur headed in her direction. She dodged the foot, taking the blow on the shoulder. That arm went numb to the fingers, and she ended up sprawled across her good arm. Twisted around so, she couldn't get away when that foot headed her way again.

Before the VC could kick her, George Lancaster rammed into the squad leader, knocking the two of them off the trail. They tripped over each other—Lancaster's hands tied behind his back and the squad leader with the radio on his back—and went down in a heap. Viet Cong rushed over. Three of them pulled the squad leader to his feet while two others clubbed Lancaster into submission.

"Stop it!" yelled Casey as she threw up a hand and crawled on top of Lancaster. "Get away from him!" Hands jerked her to her feet, then those same hands grabbed her arms, pulling them behind her back where they were re-tied.

Casey shuddered. For a moment she had lost her objectivity, had forgotten that this wasn't her war to fight—only to report, and she damned well better remember that. Her face ached; she deserved the pain, deserved the salty taste of blood in her mouth. Any more foolishness like that and she might never live to see Hanoi. The Vietnamese didn't need Casey Blackburn to report this story to the world.

One of the guerrillas was reasoning with the squad leader, saying Gzap couldn't possibly execute a Party hero for the loss of a radio, and that was just what the squad leader would be when he returned to the base camp: a Party hero. The broken radio was of no consequence.

The squad leader glanced at the woman, nodded, and ordered a man into the jungle to recover the handset. He spoke sharply up and down the trail, telling his men to prepare to move out and assigning those who would carry the stretcher. After that, he sauntered over to Casey. Before he reached her, his hand snaked out, slapping her head one way, then the other.

Casey's legs gave way and she went to her knees. Lights flashed, her ears rung, and blood oozed from the corner of her mouth. Tears ran down her cheeks. She had to bite her tongue to keep from screaming.

"Stop that!" ordered Falcon in Vietnamese from his stretcher.

The squad leader stopped in mid-swing, about to club the woman over the head with his fist. He stared at the American lying on the stretcher, hands tied behind his back. Falcon stared right back.

The two men glared at each other until the man sent to find the handset shouted he had found the thing and held it up. The squad leader lowered his hand and appeared to forget all about the two Americans.

One of the guerrillas pulled Casey to her feet and

held her there. For Casey everything was a blur. Oh, Lord, how she wanted to pass out. She was so tired, her face ached, and her legs were unsteady.

The Viet Cong returned from the darkness of the jungle floor with the handset. When the squad leader reached for it, he got a knife in the chest instead. At least that's what Casey thought she saw. She couldn't be sure. One of the squad leader's own men turning on the bastard was what she wanted to see.

Casey blinked as the squad leader slid off the knife and dropped to the dusk of the jungle floor. She turned to her guard. Had the guard seen anything? No. The guard had seen nothing. Blood gushed from his slit throat. His eyes were glazed over, and he, too, was on his way to the ground. Casey looked around. What was going on?

Someone was behind her! With a knife! She could feel the blade near her tied hands. When she gasped, a hand covered her mouth, cutting off her scream.

"Quiet!" whispered a voice, a voice with a flat, Southern accent, an accent like her father's.

In her heart of hearts, Casey had always known her father wasn't dead, and that's why she was here, to find her daddy and bring him home. Instead, he had found her. Daddy would know how to deal with these bastards—yes, he would!

The hand came away from her mouth and a knife sliced the rope off her wrists. Casey glanced behind her and saw a tall man with green and black stripes across his face. He, too, wore black pajamas. The man was too tall to be her daddy and much too young. Now the tall man was steering her away from the VC. Shouldn't they be running?

"Who are you?" asked Casey.

"Quiet," whispered the man again with the same Southern accent. This was so weird.

"But Lancaster—"

"Stop here!"

What else could she do? Whoever he was, the man certainly knew how to hold onto a person's arm.

When they stopped, Falcon passed them, moving down the trail and leaning into another man who wore black pajamas and had green and black greasepaint on his face, too.

The tall man squeezed Casey's arm. "Follow them, lady, and when the shooting starts, keep moving. No matter how scared you are."

Casey nodded dumbly.

The man let go and disappeared in the darkness, in the direction of the Viet Cong. Only then did Casey become aware of how much she'd depended on the tall man to remain on her feet.

"Get up here!" came a hoarse whisper from the man helping Falcon along.

Behind Casey, a scream broke the stillness of the jungle night. Men shouted and automatic weapons clattered. Bullets mixed with red tracers flew up the trail. Casey dropped to the ground as the boom of a shotgun drowned out the *rat-a-tat-tat* of automatic rifle fire.

She glanced up the trail and realized that the general and his helper had disappeared in the darkness ahead of her. What had the tall man said? Keep moving. Keep moving no matter how scared you are. He had been right. Any minute Charlie would be after her, and this time they'd do more than slap her around.

Casey scrambled to her feet and ran until she caught up with Falcon and his helper. She put a shoulder under Falcon's arm so they could move along.

Now why'd she done that? Wouldn't it make more sense to run on alone? And run like hell?

"What's happening?" asked Falcon, stumbling along.

"Charlie's coming!" answered his helper. "We've got to haul ass! Sir!"

A bullet flew overhead. Everyone ducked, including Falcon. His reaction wasn't lost on the helper. He looked across Falcon to Casey.

"Can you take him? I need to go back."

"Go back?" Was the man nuts? Couldn't he hear what was going on back there?

"Sure! There's only Blue Jay and Willie Tee, and you had another wounded, didn't you? That doesn't leave many hands free to return fire."

"Go!" ordered Falcon and shook the man off.

The helper didn't hesitate but ran back down the trail. Falcon tried to run alone but stumbled and went down. Casey helped him to his feet.

"Sorry to get you into this, Casey," said the general, after he was on his feet once again.

"Er—yes, sir," said Casey as they started out again. "But maybe it'd be best if we discussed this matter at a later date."

"Yes—perhaps it would."

If the helper was right, reasoned Casey, only three

Americans stood between her and ten to fifteen VC. Make that twelve Viet Cong. She'd counted them for her story.

Casey wanted to laugh. That wasn't a story happening back there, but men fighting for their lives—and her chance for reporting what had happened. And when those three GIs were dead, how long would it take the VC to catch up with a middle-aged man and an exhausted woman?

Not long. Not long at all.

CHAPTER
EIGHT

Robert Sligh sat in the rooftop bar of the Carevelle Hotel in downtown Saigon and cursed his twin devils: television and his own newspaper's editors.

Damn! If his editors didn't believe his stories, they should come over here and check them out themselves. But they wouldn't. They didn't have the nerve, and that's why they were editors and he was reporting from the field.

Dammit! There was nothing wrong with his stories. They just didn't fit his editors' preconceived ideas of this war, and that made Sligh wrong, not his editors, nor the god-almighty president of the United States.

No. Never! The president and his generals could do no wrong. Not when defending the Republic against godless communism. And as long as those dumb-asses didn't print his stories—as they were—television would grab all the headlines. Why couldn't his editors see television was muscling in on the biggest story since Korea?

Because his editors were still comparing Vietnam to Korea. Shit, the Korean War would be a fucking footnote after this fiasco was over. Talk about generals fighting today's war with yesterday's strategy—sometimes his editors made the generals look positively brilliant.

Sometimes.

Sligh finished his drink and ordered another. Now was the time to get the jump on television. TV didn't have a clue as to what was happening. Hell, none of the networks even had a bureau in Saigon until the president began sending American boys over here to die. As far as TV was concerned, little yellow boys could die here until hell froze over and the networks still wouldn't cover this frigging war. That was left to the print media . . . until the damn story was worthy enough for TV.

Damn TV! He hadn't worked his way up from a cub reporter to be upstaged—yes, that was the word!—upstaged by some fool whose standard equipment for a war zone included a damn hair dryer.

Sligh stared in the mirror behind the bar. Funny, he'd never noticed that extra gray, but the jowls had always been there, along with the smudges under the eyes. And the nose. Hell, Sligh, you're too damn ugly to do analysis—even for TV.

Sligh whirled around on his bar stool and surveyed the reporters gathering for their regular Friday night of lying, drinking, and arguing—arguing over where to find the best whores in this lousy city. Sligh didn't have a friend among them, and not because he couldn't lie, drink, or whore with the best of them. They were all

lazy bastards, only marginally better than TV reporters. These print journalists—journalists, hell!—they
wouldn't get off their duffs and get out into the field
where the real stories were. Instead, they let the army
spoon-feed them everything the army wanted them to
know. Lies! Everything the army told you was lies. The
army was filled with liars, and anyone who believed
what the army had to say, about this war or anything
else, wasn't much of a reporter.

He scanned the room. Where was Casey Blackburn?
Now there was a girl who caught on fast, and Casey
Blackburn would talk with old Robert, not leave him
sitting alone at the bar. Hell, the girl listened better
than his wife. Another reason why he worked overseas.

Casey wanted to know the score, even if it was for
all the wrong reasons. Just because your daddy had
died here wasn't reason enough to understand this war,
and just because more American boys would die here
was no good reason either. American boys had been
marching off and dying for generations—without questioning what they were marching off and dying for! The
fools deserved to die! Maybe the girl's father most of
all. According to Casey, her father had volunteered for
every dirty little war to come along until it had finally
gotten him killed.

Old Robert would teach young Casey a thing or two.
Old Robert would teach her that it didn't matter who
won or lost these silly-ass wars, who fought or died, or
even where the hell they were fought, but who received
the byline. When your name was on the byline, you

had a chance to become somebody, and with your name on a really big story, that put you beyond the reach of mere editors.

Yes. Old Robert had lots of stuff to teach young Casey Blackburn. Not to mention there was always the chance he'd bed her. Wasn't there something about girls who lost their daddies, something about them searching for their daddy until they found him in the bed of an older man?

A barmaid interrupted Sligh's speculations about how a naked Casey Blackburn might look and how she might perform in bed. "Telephone, Mr. Sligh."

The reporter downed his drink, threw some money on the bar, pulled his heavy frame off the stool, and ambled into the hallway. When he did, several reporters looked up from their drinks and watched him go.

In the hallway was a new row of phones, a sure sign of a growing war—something else his editors couldn't see. Maybe he should send them a photograph of the phones. Then again, maybe he should pack it in. After all, he was getting a little long in the tooth to be busting his ass and getting no respect from the editorial staff.

One of the phones had been left off the hook, and when Sligh picked it up all he heard was a dial tone. No problem. His source would call back. The first time this guy had called, Sligh had almost hung up on him. Thank God he hadn't. Without a source, a reporter was nowhere, and this one was pure gold.

The day of that first call, Sligh had had his bag packed. He was leaving for the beaches of Vung Tau where a hot woman and cold beer were waiting, both changing temperature.

"You should leave town for the weekend, my friend," said an American voice over the telephone.

Leave town? What was this guy talking about? Was the hotel to be bombed again? "Actually, I *was* leaving for the beach when some asshole called."

"Wrong direction, my friend. Tay Ninh. You should spend your weekend in Tay Ninh. The ARVNs had a base camp overrun up there."

"I know. I was in the Delta collecting leeches." Sligh didn't need this shit. First it was the army, then his editors, and now any old asshole could call up and tell you what to write about this damn war.

"Tay Ninh, Mr. Sligh," the American repeated. "It's time you wrote the real story of what happened up there. That is, if you're not too drunk to do the job."

Sligh found himself cursing a dead line. "To hell with you," he said, hanging up the phone. "Friend."

The reporter picked up his bag and left for the beach. But out on the street, when he hailed a cab, it was for Long Bien where he could arrange transport to Tay Ninh City. In Tay Ninh, he learned the base camp the source had spoken of had been overrun because the ARVNs had run out of ammo. Sligh found this hard to believe with all the supplies the Americans forced on their allies. Hell, the Army of the Republic of South Vietnam was better equipped than the US Marines.

Digging deeper into the story, Sligh learned that instead of resupplying his own troops, the Vietnamese commander had sent his planes to Saigon for booze, broads, and food. So, the supply planes had been held up as their flight crews enjoyed the sights and sounds of the capital.

Saigon was hard to resist. With the arrival of the Americans there were bars on every corner, pretty girls everywhere. Sligh waited until the right editor was riding the foreign desk and slipped the story through. Then the shit hit the fan. Both governments were infuriated, and Sligh was chided by the brass to either get on the team or get out of the country. Even his editor told him to cool it.

Sligh told his editor he couldn't have it both ways. He'd have to choose between good stories or being on the White House guest list. His editor had come through loud and clear on the overseas hookup. He told Sligh no damn reporter had to tell him his business, that he had the balls to print anything Sligh dug up, but from now on all Sligh's stories were to cross *his* desk. The editor didn't believe the US Army that incompetent, the government of South Vietnam that corrupt, and wasn't about to be hung out to dry by some over-the-hill reporter. And furthermore, the first time Sligh fucked up, his ass would be on the next plane stateside. Sligh would go back to covering garden parties, if he was lucky. So, Mister Know-it-all, added the editor, make sure *you* get your facts straight because I can always get back on the White House guest list, but Robert Sligh might never find another job reporting from anywhere.

Lost in all this was the South Vietnamese general who'd caused the death of several hundred of his men.

The general couldn't be fired or demoted. He was related to the premier—whoever the hell that was this week—so the boob was reassigned to Saigon . . . where he was closer to the booze and broads.

The phone in the hallway rang and Sligh snatched it off the hook. As he did he glanced up and down the hall. A couple of reporters were smoking cigarettes outside the door to the bar.

The voice on the phone asked, "Where've you been lately, my friend?"

Sligh's source wasn't making idle conversation but speaking in code. If Sligh ticked off the locations in proper order, the source would give him another tip. But if anything was out of sequence, his source would think he had the wrong man or Sligh was too drunk to follow up the next lead. That had happened before, but Sligh wasn't about to give up drinking, not when he had to work in this damn country and compete with television.

"The Delta, mountains, and Ton Son Nhut Airport."

They weren't the last places Sligh had gathered stories, but the last three furnished by this particular source. Two had led to stories, real good ones; the third had been nothing more than political bullshit. His source pulled that every once in a while, and Sligh figured the asshole had strong connections to the anti-war movement in Berkeley.

"You should be over at Long Bien, my friend," said the voice on the phone. "They've sealed off the compound."

"What's going on?"

"That's your job to find out."

"If the compound's locked up tight, I'll need help getting in."

"That's your problem, friend, not mine."

The line went dead.

Sligh couldn't believe this guy. The army could never trace his calls. He never stayed on the line long enough. All he did was pass along the tip. It was left to Sligh to dig out the story.

Sligh hung up the phone but continued to stare at the instrument. This tip was happening now, not some snafu waiting to be uncovered months later. Did that mean his source worked inside the Long Bien compound? Maybe in the command bunker itself?

Heading for the elevator, Sligh passed reporters in the hall who nodded to him. Sligh never saw them. He was lost in thought. After waiting for the cage to arrive with its operator, Sligh stepped aboard for the ride down. When the elevator disappeared from sight, the reporters dropped their cigarettes to the floor, smushed them, and raced downstairs.

Outside the hotel Sligh took the first pedicab coming along. The pedicab wasn't headed in the right direction, but Sligh had several tails to lose. He always had a tail to lose.

Damn! Why couldn't these people dig up their own stories, or at least learn how to tail him properly? No matter. They'd be easy enough to lose. What was important was learning what the army was up to, or finding someone who could tell him. And Sligh thought he knew a man who'd be quite interested in doing just that.

Chapter Nine

C asey and Falcon were hobbling along when they heard footsteps behind them. Before they could stumble off the trail, men in black pajamas rushed out of the darkness, one of them waving an AK-47. Casey didn't know whether to hit the dirt or keep on running.

The lead figure said in English, "I told you they'd be up here."

"They'd better be," said another voice, but not the one Casey recognized as belonging to the tall man who had sliced the rope off her wrists and hurried her down the trail. "I told you to stay with him, Pike."

"And miss my chance for you to owe me one, Willie Tee? No way."

"Hold it down up there," called out the tall man, appearing out of the darkness behind the other two, "and keep this column moving."

Pike ran over and put his shoulder under the general's arm. Casey recognized him as the one who'd insisted on returning to the fire fight. Besides the black pajamas Pike wore a headband from a first-aid kit. Looking closer, Casey could make out seven skulls and crossbones on the triangular cotton patch, now soiled and dirty, the soldier's personal body count.

"Take a break, soldier."

"Thank . . . you."

"Damn! You *are* a girl! So what you doing tonight, babe? Got anything planned?"

"Ignore him, ma'am," said the man addressed as Willie Tee. He was a black man. Casey could see that despite the green and brown streaks across his face. On the black man's back was a pack and across his chest, a cloth bandolier filled with curved magazines such as the one in the man's rifle. "Pike's from New York."

"Upstate," qualified Pike as he moved ahead with Falcon.

Casey shook her head as she hurried along. She'd fallen in with a bunch of nuts, but at least they were American nuts.

"Who's got the point?" asked Pike, holding out his weapon, the shotgun Casey had heard over the *rat-a-tat-tat* of the fire fight.

"Me!" Lancaster said, and he ran by, snatching the pump-action 12-gauge out of Pike's hand to take the lead.

"You're alive!" exclaimed Casey.

"So far," Lancaster replied grimly.

"Hey," Pike said after him, "I don't know about you taking the point."

"I do! I want out of this miserable little country!"

"Then take these." Pike reached in a pocket on the legs of his black fatigues, pulled out some clothing, and threw it at him. "They'll give you an edge."

When the pajamas hit Lancaster's chest, he stopped and stared at what he had caught with his free hand. Both pieces of clothing had the durability of fatigues but were black in color. The rest of the column jogged past him as Lancaster stared at a uniform that would immediately mark him for death if the enemy captured him wearing it. Minutes later, dressed in black, he passed the others and took the point.

"Be careful," whispered Casey as, once again, he hurried by.

"Send up a rifle," Pike called over his shoulder.

Willie Tee ran forward and handed Pike an AK-47.

"You use Charlie's weapons?" asked Casey.

"Yes, ma'am," said the black man. "Would even if they didn't go with the pjs. Out here, the AK just seems to work better than the M-16. But don't tell Mr. Colt." He paused. "Going to make it, ma'am?"

"'Casey,' please, and I'll give it one hell of a try."

"That's it. I'm Willie T. Eskew, and as you've already heard, the fool with Falcon is Pike."

Casey glanced behind her. "And the tall man with the radio?"

"Lieutenant Stuart. Out here called 'Blue Jay.'"

She nodded and continued along. It was one of those silly macho things men at war did, and for the first time Casey was willing to play along.

"Truth is, Casey, this ain't gonna get any easier and

there's no way we can stop, so when you don't think you can go on, you've still gotta keep moving. When that happens, watch the ground ahead of you and concentrate on putting one foot in front of the other."

"Gotcha."

"Easy to say," Eskew said, with a grim smile, "tougher to do."

The black man jogged ahead of her, and the Americans continued along to the song of the cicadas, crickets, and Lt. Stuart's efforts trying to reach the command center at Long Bien.

"Eagle's Nest, Eagle's Nest, this is Blue Jay. Come in, Eagle's Nest." Stuart tried again and again, finally giving up with a loud "goddamn machine!"

No one called for him to hold it down; however, Pike did clear his throat loudly.

Half an hour later, Casey thought she'd die if they didn't stop, but knew it would certainly kill her if she did. Casey wanted to ask how much longer it'd be before they recrossed back into Vietnam but didn't dare. It might be longer than she could stand.

Her mouth was bone-dry. She desperately needed a drink of water. The sweat dripping off her nose didn't come close to doing the job. She was bathed in the stuff; her fatigues were soaked, clinging to her. Sweat ran down her back and across her stomach, but ahead of her, the black man ran with ease, holding his rifle chest-high, with a pack riding on his back. How'd he do it?

Eskew didn't smoke. That had to be it. The sergeant

didn't smoke, probably never had. Casey gritted her teeth and wheezed through them. No one had told her that to file one of her stories, she'd be force-marched through the jungle. If her editor could see her now . . . .

Gil would laugh his ass off. Gil ran in marathons on weekends. You had to be crazy to run marathons. Marathons were over twenty miles long. Casey tried to ignore the stitch that had begun in one side, had moved to the other, and now was in both sides. Why hadn't she been crazy enough to take up marathon running?

One thing for sure: If she got out of this alive, she was giving up smoking. No more cigarettes. Not a damn one. She was giving up cigarettes the moment she walked, or crawled, out of this frigging jungle. Matter of fact, she'd give them up as of now.

Casey glanced at the jungle roof. Did you hear that, God? No more smoking. Absolutely none, if you get me out of this alive. And pass along some water while you're at it. Maybe let it rain. That'd do the job. She could handle some rain. And she wouldn't even have to stop. She'd had plenty of practice collecting the moisture dripping off her nose.

With a burst of energy born of desperation, Casey sprinted up beside the black man who wore equipment she recognized from her long hours in base camp: web harness, first-aid pouch, knife, fragmentation grenades, smoke grenades, strobe lights, Claymore mines, canteens, a pack-load of extra magazines, and the rifle. None of which rattled or reflected light.

Gasping, Casey asked, "Willie . . . how much longer . . . before we return to Vietnam?"

"Not headed for 'Nam, Casey. Running further west, heading into Cambodia."

"Wh—what?" Casey stumbled, almost fell, and had to run hard to catch up. "Why?"

"Back where we picked you up, Charlie had the trail blocked toward 'Nam, so into Cambodia we go."

"But—but we could run into more Viet Cong."

"Doubt that. More likely NVA." Eskew set his jaw. "The real tough bastards."

* * *

An American airborne unit penetrated the jungle canopy ten minutes after the firefight concluded between the Viet Cong and the Blue Jay Team on the east-west trail. They did it by dropping a two-and-a-half-ton truck from two thousand feet over the crash site. The deuce and a half also carried several fifty-gallon drums of grease strapped in the rear of the truck. Using the air force's infrared photographs, they were able to punch a hole within fifty yards of the downed chopper.

The American captain had his men secure the crash site, sent out patrols, and reported his findings to Long Bien. "Eagle's Nest, this is Pathfinder. I have two dead pilots and no sign of Falcon. Neither pilot was killed in the crash but shot in the back of the head."

"Murdered?" The shocked voice of the officer of the day carried across the command net to anyone listening.

"I don't think Charlie wanted to be slowed down by our injured."

"Then Charlie has the two reporters, Falcon, and his aide."

"And the man you sent down in the hoist."

In the command center, Daniels gripped the communications console. This couldn't be happening. A crash he could take, even the death of Falcon, but the CIC captured by the Vietnamese? How had the bastards gotten there so fast?

They must have had men in the area. That had to be it. Damn the luck! And from one end of Vietnam to the other, even back in the Pentagon, people were listening in to how he was going about rescuing Falcon.

Daniels glanced at the clock. His unit had arrived less than forty-five minutes after the crash. No one could fault him on that. But they would. He was the officer of the day. Daniels swallowed hard. A routine rescue mission had suddenly turned into a career-buster. There'd been no blemishes on his record until this, but now, because he'd been the man on duty, the man in charge, the one responsible . . . .

Daniels realized everyone in the bunker was staring at him, some with pity in their eyes. He ran his tongue around the inside of his mouth to find enough saliva to speak to his man on the ground at the crash site.

"We have to assume the survivors who could walk away from the crash site are still alive. The exception would be Falcon, whom they'd carry out dead or alive. Pathfinder, abandon the crash site. We have backup in the air and on its way. Move to the east-west trail and pick up Charlie's trail. Then hotfoot it after him. You'll be the hammer. I'll set up the blocking force ahead of them. And I want some of your men to sweep the left and right sides of the trail, and don't forget to assign sweepers to trail you."

"Wilco. Pathfinder. Out."

The OD stared at the phone. Daniels wanted to smash the son of a bitch against the console. Instead, he gripped the instrument tightly and stared at the map across the room. The damn jungle was crawling with Charlies. And why not? This was one of their major infiltration routes into South Vietnam.

Damn! When were the good guys going to get a break?

Daniels chewed his lip again.

If Falcon's still alive, that's the only break we need. We'll make all the others—even if we have to kill Falcon in the process. Better Falcon dead than on TV with the Russkis giving Uncle Ho an around-the-world hookup.

Daniels realized how quiet it had become in the command bunker. The clicking of a teletype, the hum of the IBM computers—besides that, nothing. Funny how no one had any suggestions at these moments.

Daniels turned to Manley. "Is the other unit ready for insertion?"

"Yes, sir. Hovering over the crash site with more trucks, just waiting for a target."

The OD stared at the map on the far wall. "Target alpha will be five miles south of the North Vietnamese base camp—to cut off any reinforcements headed for the crash site, and . . . ." The OD gestured at the map. "Target bravo will be the trail junction at the base of Magic Mountain. The unit at landing zone bravo will be the anvil for Pathfinder's hammer."

"Want either site prepped before the landing?" called the artillery liaison from across the room.

"Absolutely not. Our men must have the element of surprise. Manley, once you've assigned targets to each company, get their backups in the air. Have them rendezvous over their respective LZs."

"Yes, sir."

But before the unit hovering over the crash site could be inserted, the company commander reported six dead Viet Cong from his location on the east-west trail. "Two were killed by small arms fire; another two had their throats cut. The RTO was stabbed in the chest and the last Charlie was blown away by a shotgun."

The air force liaison looked from the speaker to the communications console. "Charlie fighting over the spoils of war, wanting to be the one to bring Falcon in?"

"Not with a shotgun, they weren't."

"Blue Jay," Manley said. "He sandbagged his position."

The artillery liaison snorted. "Good way to have artillery dropped on your ass, us not knowing where you are. The man's obviously a grandstander. That's all we need out there with Falcon."

"Right now, I'll take anything I can get." The OD had returned to staring at the map at the end of the room.

"We've got to get those Americans out of Cambodia," said someone. "It's against the rules of engagement for Americans to cross the border."

"Okay, let's wrap this up." To the company commander on the east-west trail, Daniels said, "Pathfinder, form up and move back in our direction. Send a squad ahead of you to catch up with Blue Jay. It's only a five or six-man recon team, and we don't—"

"Three-man," corrected Manley, looking at his computer screen. "Cortez bought the farm last time out."

"And Blue Jay went out without a replacement? Who is this guy anyway?"

"Lieutenant James Stuart, sir," Manley said, reading from a computer printout. "His lurp team has the highest body count of any recon team in the last four months."

Daniels nodded. That would mean that four months ago, James Stuart's commander had begun employing the Blue Jay Team as a hunter-killer team, instead of exclusively gathering intelligence. "Sparkman, get Blue Jay on the horn. I want to talk to this man, especially about not knowing he was already across the border when we initially communicated."

Sparkman shook his head. "I've tried, sir, but for some reason the Blue Jay Team doesn't respond."

CHAPTER
TEN

Less than twenty-five yards ahead of the Blue Jay Team, Sergeant George F. Lancaster hurried along on point, his finger nervously running up and down the trigger guard of the pump-action shotgun. It was darker than night in this dad-blame jungle. Only the rutted-out trail and the illuminated dial of his compass made it possible for him to find his way. And if Charlie appeared out of the darkness all he could hope for was that the black pajamas would give him the edge Pike had said they would. He hadn't wanted to wear the enemy's uniform, but what the heck, with Falcon in tow they couldn't consider recapture.

Only yards ahead of Lancaster, a Vietnamese point man materialized out of the darkness. Lancaster slowed to a walk as the enemy's rifle came up. As are all soldiers, the Vietnamese was hesitant to fire until he could identify the shadowy figure as one of the enemy. After all, they were on *his* side of the border.

Lancaster's shoulders tightened. He all but stopped breathing but forced himself forward, shotgun draped casually across his arm. He'd been talking to himself, preparing himself for just such a moment . . . .

There's nothing to be afraid of, Charlie. Can't you see my pj's? I'm one of you. Just one of the guys. Let me get a little closer. Just a little closer, you son of a gun. Just a little bit closer . . . .

Lancaster couldn't warn those behind him, nor did they expect him to. By warning the rest of the team, he would only give them away. Everyone's chances were greatly improved with every second he closed with the enemy.

Just a little bit closer, Charlie. Just a little bit closer . . . .

This was no different from coming down through the jungle canopy in the hoist. Once again he was the point man, and the point man's job was to be the shock troops for the trailing column.

Just a little bit closer, you son of a gun. Just a little bit—

The Charlie stopped.

What's he doing? Oh, no! He's turning around to tell the others someone's ahead of them on the trail!

Lancaster saw he wasn't going to be quick enough and knew he couldn't use the shotgun. "Hey, you!"

The Vietnamese turned around, hardly believing what he had heard. Now he could see Lancaster's white face, the larger build, and the shotgun in the American's hands. The Vietnamese opened his mouth to warn those behind him, and Lancaster shut it with an upward swing of the shotgun butt. The blow shattered the Vietnamese's jaw and sent pieces of bone flying into the man's brain. The VC was lifted off his feet, soared through the air, and was dead before he hit the side of the trail.

Lancaster didn't wait to see him fall. He continued moving forward, toward the others that had to be there. But was he charging into a squad, a platoon, or a company of Charlies? Remember the lurp patrol that mistakenly took on the point man of a North Vietnamese battalion? Sweet Jesus! That'd happened up north while he'd been working the Delta. Now he was up north, running with the Blue Jay Team—a lurp patrol. First Sergeant, I wasn't meant to get out of this miserable little country alive.

The column of sappers, the unit sent to blow bridges in South Vietnam, was twenty paces behind their point man, and once again Lancaster was mistaken for one of them. Lancaster clubbed the first man as he had the point man and sent him flying. Silence was still his best ally, and he intended to use it as long as possible.

Lancaster's next victim couldn't understand why one Vietnamese would be attacking another. While the sapper was trying to figure this out, Lancaster dropped him with a single blow. But it wasn't a clean kill, and the sapper screamed bloody murder as he went down.

Well, his luck couldn't last forever. Lancaster opened up on the next man with the shotgun, and he was so close that the blast ripped the Vietnamese apart. The Vietnamese behind that man was splattered with blood, pieces of flesh, and pellets of shot. The splattered man looked down to see what had hit him . . . and found a shotgun jammed in *his* stomach.

Lancaster blew this man across the trail. The Vietnamese collapsed against a tree with his head sagging over the remains of his chest. The next Charlie got off a single shot before Lancaster blew the man's head off. A bullet zinged by his ear.

Dammit! I'm a dead man! Good-bye, Judy. Good-bye boys. Fuck the army! And Lancaster ran down the trail screaming "Fuck the army," over and over again.

The next sapper fired off several shots at the approaching figure. All missed. Lancaster couldn't miss with the shotgun and blew off the man's arm. The Vietnamese fell to the ground, screaming and fumbling around for his missing arm. Lancaster shoved the injured man out of his way and hurried down the trail toward the next one. The next one? The next one! Good God! How many were there?

The sapper in the middle of the column always carried his rifle on automatic. He had been warned not to do so as he might accidentally shoot a member of his own squad. When he heard the booming of the shotgun, the automatic weapons fire, and the screams ahead of him, he opened up on anyone and anything ahead of him.

His burst caught the sapper in front of him across the back, propelling the injured man up the trail and shielding Lancaster from most of the bullets. One, however, plowed a furrow up Lancaster's forearm into the upper arm, shattering that arm and causing Lancaster to drop his weapon. A second drilled a hole through the loose part of his black pj's, a third smashed into his rib cage. Lancaster was twisted to one side. He tripped over the rutted out trail and went into a roll, dragging his good hand behind him as he fumbled around for the shotgun. Did the man following him know the drill? "Fire, fire, fire!" he shouted.

Pike ran forward, rifle on automatic, and holding the rifle waist-high so he wouldn't hit Lancaster who, if this was done correctly, should be hugging the ground. Pike hosed down the trail ahead of him, and after running out of ammo, reversed his clip—a second clip was taped to the first and upside down—and fired another burst. Pike didn't know how many Charlies there were, but after surprising the enemy, you leaned on your advantage with more and more firepower. Pike screamed as he ran down the trail, to give the sappers the impression they were being charged by a madman armed with a machine gun.

The remaining members of the sapper unit were stunned. Why were they being attacked on this side of the border? It must be some mistake. But that mistake was killing them and killing them fast. When Pike changed clips, creating a lull in the firing, one of the survivors pulled his companions down beside him, forming an impromptu skirmish line. The three sappers shrugged out of their packs filled with explosives meant for the bridges of South Vietnam and fired into the darkness—until the man in the middle, the one who had organized them, was blown away.

Lancaster had found the shotgun.

The sappers to the left and right were sprayed with pellets, and it broke them. They leaped to their feet, turned, and ran in the direction from which they had just come. Now it became a footrace to see which one of the two could return to the base camp before the other. When one of them stumbled, the other man shoved him out of the way and ran past him. Seconds later, Pike came out of the darkness and shot the unlucky man getting to his feet, then continued down the trail after any remaining Vietnamese who might be left. This deep in Cambodia, they couldn't afford to let even one of the Charlies get away.

Pike ran until he was satisfied he'd killed all the bastards, then stopped and listened. Did he hear something ahead of him? He wasn't sure. Hell, if you listened long enough you could hear just about anything out here. Certain he'd killed them all, Pike waited for the rest of his team to join him. It was a chance to catch his breath, and Pike didn't dare go back. He might be mistaken for the enemy. Wearing the black pajamas cut both ways.

Ahead of Pike, the surviving sapper ran in a mad panic, bouncing off vines, tripping over logs, but always leaping to his feet and running in the direction of the trail junction at the base of Magic Mountain. The Vietnamese had no idea what his squad had run into and had little curiosity to find out.

At the first blast of the shotgun, Casey dropped to the ground. Before she could scramble off the trail, Stuart was beside her, pulling her to her feet.

"Get up, lady! We're going through!"

"Going through?"

"Yes—this will only encourage the ones behind us."

"The ones behind us?"

"You don't think we killed all those Charlies back at the crash site, do you?"

Casey didn't know what to think, and before she could answer, Stuart shoved her in the direction of the shotgun blasts.

"Run, woman! Run!" Stuart stepped off the trail to wait for those who had been encouraged to renew their pursuit.

Casey stumbled down the trail, and when she glanced back to see if the VC were gaining on her, she tripped over one of the dead sappers. She somersaulted head over heels and landed sitting up and face-to-face with a Viet Cong who was propped against a tree. The VC appeared to be studying the hole in his chest.

The hole in his chest!

There was a hole in the man's chest large enough to stick your hand through. The Viet Cong's stomach, liver, and spleen had been ruptured. They had emulsified, then oozed into his lap. When Casey screamed, Stuart appeared out of the darkness and pulled her to her feet again.

"I'm not going to keep doing this. Now get moving!"

Casey pulled her gaze from the dead man and walked, then jogged down the trail. Her stomach was in turmoil. She needed to stop, but when she did, the trail behind her erupted in another firefight: Stuart versus the remaining VC from the crash site.

The VC were right behind them! How long could he hold them off?

With a burst of energy she didn't know she had, Casey caught up with Sergeant Eskew, who was helping Falcon along. She grabbed the general's other side and discovered it wasn't Falcon but George Lancaster.

When Lancaster cried out in pain, Casey jerked back, her hand coming away sticky wet. "You're hurt!"

"I can guarantee . . . it's more than hurt."

Casey flushed. She didn't know how to grab onto Lancaster to help him down the trail. Judging by the sticky fluid on her hand, blood was leaking from the man's side. One of the sergeant's arms flopped around uselessly.

Casey stopped to wipe the blood away and something foul rose in her throat. To her left was a Vietnamese with an arm ripped away, to her right, a man with his head blown off. Casey stumbled off the trail and threw up, having to hold onto a tree to finish the job. Her legs trembled and the foul taste wouldn't go away, no matter how often she cleared her throat.

She couldn't go on. She was so weak she was going to collapse in the middle of . . . in the middle of all these dead men.

Not here. She had to go on. She had to get away from this place. Behind her the shooting had stopped, and with Stuart dead, there was no one between her and the Viet Cong determined to recapture Falcon— VC who would kill anyone who got in their way. And Casey Blackburn was in their way.

Casey pushed herself off the tree, stepped around

another dead man, and forced herself to walk down the trail, then began jogging. Her father had been right. She didn't have the nerve for what he did. With her first taste of combat, she'd puked up whatever guts she had and left them somewhere along that corpse-strewn trail behind her.

CHAPTER
ELEVEN

Robert Sligh had his third pedicab drop him off in front of a hut across the road from the American command center in Long Bien. The road between the hut and command center was as wide as a four-lane highway but made of dirt. As you approached the compound you encountered first the barbed wire, then an open space filled with land mines, and finally the walls of sandbags with their towers and guards.

Sligh had already confirmed he wouldn't be allowed inside the compound no matter how much money he offered the guards. The GIs told him to get lost.

Get lost, hell! He'd show them lost. He had the last of the pedicabs turn off on a narrow lane across from the compound.

Sligh was no sooner out of the pedicab than he was mobbed by children of every size, age, and sex begging for gum, chocolates, or cigarettes, but mostly for money. Sligh fought his way to the hut, the children pulling at his shirt, the bolder ones sticking their hands inside his pockets. He slapped their hands away and hurried inside.

Goddammit! We're turning this country into a nation of beggars, not democrats.

The hut, built of wood and corrugated metal, contained a single room with a dirt floor and a bed fashioned out of bamboo. The mattress consisted of long slivers of bamboo woven together the width and length of the bed. A fan oscillated from the top of an empty ammo box, and in another corner Vietnamese music played on a radio. This was a special hut. This hut had electricity.

In the rear sat an old Vietnamese man sewing patches on American uniforms. In contrast to the electric fan and radio, the man's sewing machine was operated by pedal power. Over his head hung a naked light bulb, and stacked on tables, chairs, and boxes were more American uniforms with patches pinned or sewn on in their proper positions.

Seeing the reporter enter the hut, the tailor smiled, revealing teeth yellowed and blackened. He spit red juice on the floor. "You have sewing for me, Mr. Sligh?"

The tailor had never sewn so much as a stitch for the reporter. "May I sit down, Mr. Thieu?"

Thieu leaped from his chair. He shoved uniforms off another and set the chair out for his visitor. "Sit here. It is a great honor to have you in my house. Would you like something to drink? A beer? A Coca-Cola?"

"There's no time." Sligh pulled the chair over near where the man worked and sat down. "I need your help."

The Vietnamese nodded, sitting cross-legged in his chair. "Certainly, Mr. Sligh. Whatever I can do."

"I need to get inside the American compound and I need to do it tonight."

The tailor seemed genuinely puzzled. "You cannot do this yourself?"

"They won't let me inside."

"Then how can I help?"

"I have no time for games, Thieu."

The tailor glanced at his window. The sound of military vehicles grinding down the four-lane road floated inside; dust followed, drifting through the open window. Everything in the hut was covered with a light coat of dust.

"Mr. Sligh, what you ask is very dangerous. Only a short time ago all my people were sent home. No one is allowed inside the compound except Americans. Something very strange is happening in there. Do you know what it is?"

"Yes," lied the reporter, "and that's why I need to get inside."

"I am only a humble tailor. There is a difference between what I know and what I can do."

"Mr. Thieu, I've been in your country long enough to know who can help me and who can't . . . or won't. Are you saying you won't?"

"I am saying I cannot."

"Nevertheless, I will return in one hour." Sligh got to his feet.

"And why would you do that?"

"Mr. Thieu, don't play games. I know for a fact you've

lost two sons and a brother in this war. They died fighting with the Viet Cong, so don't tell me you can't put me in touch with the right people." At the door he stopped and turned around. "One thing I can tell you is that the right people aren't going to be very happy if I don't get inside that compound tonight."

*　　*　　*

Pike was signaling his position with birdcalls. The first person up the trail was Falcon, who didn't know anything about birdcalls but did know how to use an AK-47. He'd taken the rifle and its ammo off one of the dead sappers and followed Pike down the trail.

When Falcon limped by, Pike whispered, "Hey! Wait up!"

Falcon whirled around and Pike hit the dirt.

"No! Don't shoot! It's me, Pike!"

Falcon lowered his rifle and limped over to where the point man was getting to his feet.

"The birdcalls are signals?"

"Yes, sir, but I doubt you can hear them in Long Bien with all those generators running."

"I can't say I can, but I'm out here now so I'd better learn."

Pike smiled. "You won't get a chance, sir. We'll have you back in Long Bien in time for tonight's movie."

Falcon didn't return the smile. He wasn't so sure. It'd been years since he'd spent any time in the field, and like all garrison soldiers, he had a tendency to overestimate the enemy's ability.

121

Casey Blackburn and Sergeant Eskew jogged out of the darkness with Lancaster. Falcon slung his rifle over his shoulder to help them ease the wounded man to the ground.

"Third time's the charm," groaned Lancaster, remembering the previous firefights from which he had escaped unscathed.

"What's that?" asked Falcon.

"Nothing, sir. Private joke."

Turning his attention to Blackburn, Falcon said, "You're looking good, Casey."

An embarrassed smile crept across Casey's face. She wasn't worried about herself but Lancaster. He had come all the way down through the jungle canopy to rescue her, only to be shot for his trouble. It wasn't fair, not fair at all.

"Keep him upright," Eskew said. "Pike, move down the trail. I have plenty of help here."

Pike groused as he disappeared. "You know how I hate to be alone in the dark."

Eskew laid a muffled red flashlight in front of Lancaster, then ripped off the pajama top and the man's fatigue blouse. "The supply sergeant's not going to be very happy with the way you've been treating your new uniform, soldier."

Lancaster smiled weakly. "I thought the pjs made me invincible."

Eskew unbuttoned the shirt. "They don't even do that for Charlie." He peeled the shirt down to Lancaster's waist.

Lt. Stuart arrived. He swung his web gear and the radio off his back and to the ground. His uniform was the same as the others: the black pajamas, as well as a "boonie" cap, a camouflage hat with a shapeless brim that could be stuck in a pocket or used to grasp a hot rifle barrel. "Less than a minute, Willie Tee."

"Plenty of time for hands like mine."

"But that's not what you usually use them for," said Pike from farther up the trail.

"Watch your language, men," cautioned Falcon. "There's a lady out here."

Eskew smiled at Casey hunched down on the other side of Lancaster. "Okay, lady, since you're here, hold him upright. That'll free Falcon for rear guard. About twenty feet down the trail, sir."

"Right." Falcon stood up, and using the butt of his rifle as a crutch, he limped off into the darkness.

Eskew watched him go. "Might have a problem there."

Stuart was wrapping a bandanna around one of his thighs. The one with the blood running down it. "We'll worry about that when it becomes a problem."

Eskew focused the muffled light on the work Lt. Stuart was doing on himself. "Going to need some of mother's magic over there?"

Stuart tied off the bandanna, then went to work on the radio. "It's only a scratch."

"Then I hope you've had all your shots." The black man fished a bandage from his first-aid kit, ripped the plastic off, and shook it out. Four strings were attached to a pad smaller than a sanitary napkin that he placed over the hole in Lancaster's side. When Eskew tied the strings around the wounded man's torso, Lancaster stiffened and clenched his teeth.

"All in all . . . I think I'd rather bleed to death."

"I've had the same feeling—when working on myself."

"Will he be all right?" asked Casey, chewing her lip. She was on her knees now, one hand holding Lancaster's good arm, the other supporting the wounded man's back.

"Boy like Lancaster's too tough to kill." Eskew took out another patch, ripped off the plastic, and shook the strings loose again. "Right, Lancaster?"

"But Charlie keeps trying."

"Riding 'Heroes Patrol.' You must've been somebody, somewhere, sometime."

"That . . . was then." Lancaster grimaced in pain. "This is . . . now."

"Where you from?" asked Eskew, as he went to work on the wounded arm.

"West . . . Texas. You?" asked Lancaster before involuntarily calling out, "Oh, my God!"

After dousing the injured man's arm with antiseptic, Eskew wrapped the long wound with surgical tape where the bullet had run up Lancaster's forearm. "Sorry. No time for stitches."

"Thank God . . . for that."

Eskew answered Lancaster's original question. "I'm a cracker from Georgia."

From out of the darkness up the trail, Pike said, "Don't you wish."

Casey could only watch and listen. These men could joke and laugh as they patched up their wounded. No wonder they called home the Real World. This was unreal. Totally.

Stuart cursed the radio, then sat on the ground to fasten the web gear holding his rucksack over his shoulders and around his waist. He rolled over on his hands and knees to get to his feet. "Well, if the USO show is over, we need to get moving." The strap of the whip antenna was hooked down, and there appeared to be an even longer antenna folded up and strapped across the top of the radio that sat astride the lieutenant's rucksack.

After recalling Falcon and Pike from sentry duty, Eskew looked up at Stuart. "Drugs?"

"Give him a quarter-grain. We need him on his feet."

From around his neck, Eskew pulled out his dog tags. In a holder on the chain was a small collapsible tube fitted with a hypodermic needle. Quickly the needle went into the nipple end, the needle into Lancaster's good arm, and the Syrette rolled down like a tube being emptied of toothpaste.

Stuart and Falcon were staring into the darkness behind them. The lieutenant said, "Let's get him on his feet. We're moving out."

"Can you give him time for the morphine—"

Casey was cut off as Stuart and Eskew roughly hauled Lancaster to his feet. The injured man's face became a white spot in the darkness. His legs wobbled.

Casey clutched Lancaster to keep him on his feet. "You're right, Blue Jay, this man's ready to be force-marched across Cambodia."

"He'll be just fine when the morphine kicks in," said Eskew. "Won't you, Lancaster?"

"All in all, I—I think I'd rather pass out."

Casey was glaring at Stuart. She wanted to slap the lieutenant's streaked green-and-black face.

Eskew thrust a rifle between the two of them. "I picked it up just for you."

Casey stepped back, bringing up her hands. "I can't. I'm a journalist."

Pike laughed. "Don't split hairs, lady. Charlie won't."

Eskew slung the weapon over his shoulder. "No sweat. I can always use a spare."

"Hang onto that, Willie Tee. It won't be long before she'll be begging for it."

"Take the point, Pike, and move out."

Pike groaned. "When am I going to learn to keep my big mouth shut?"

They formed up, Falcon falling in behind Pike, Lancaster behind him. Eskew handed a rubber canteen to Casey and she swished the bile out of her mouth and spit out water before taking a second pull on the canteen.

"Upset stomach?" Eskew asked softly as he stored away the canteen on his web belt.

Casey flushed, then nodded, remembering the tree she'd leaned against, clutching the barrel-shaped thing and puking her guts out.

"You're doing better than my first time out." The sergeant took a foil packed from his blouse pocket and ripped it open. "I wet my pants."

Casey smiled, not believing a word but appreciating the gesture. "Thanks, Willie Tee."

The black man was handing her a candy wafer when Stuart announced, "No stops until Magic Mountain."

"Is that where we catch a chopper?" asked Casey.

Stuart shook his head. "Not with this radio."

A shiver ran through Casey and she almost dropped her candy bar. "Then where?"

"At Magic Mountain we head south."

Remembering the photographs and maps Falcon had shown her, Casey stammered, "But—but that won't take us back to Vietnam."

Pike laughed. "Want that rifle now, lady?"

CHAPTER
TWELVE

North Vietnamese platoon leader Bien brought his men down the trail toward Magic Mountain at the double time. Bien was determined to arrive at the crash site before Colonel Gzap expected him. Quick action like that made a man's reputation. Bien smiled grimly. And he would arrive at the crash site before those fools who had captured the general found a way to lose him, as the Viet Cong would certainly do if he was not there.

Bien's furious pace made his men curse and wonder why they did not ask for a transfer out of this crazy platoon. Everyone who asked to leave received a transfer, the lieutenant letting them go with a sneer. Bien paid little attention to his men's muttering. The way Bien figured it, it was his job to set the pace, his men's to grumble about it. Over the past few years, Bien had molded this platoon in his image and resisted all attempts to break it up. If you broke up his platoon and spread it throughout the battalion, the result would not be better platoons but one less good one: his. It had been his lucky day when Colonel Gzap had taken charge of the battalion, taken charge of the mess left behind by his predecessor. The whole army had been better off with the death of that fool.

With Gzap, Bien acquired a leader who recognized Bien's high standards, and the pressure to break up his platoon ceased. Then came a new kind of pressure: Bien had to prove, over and over again, that his platoon deserved to stay together. Tonight was just such an opportunity. Bien would take charge of the American general and return him to the base camp no matter how many men fell out along the way. He would do the job even if he had to do it by himself.

There was a yelp, then a yell, at the head of the column three or four men ahead of Bien. The lieutenant harrumphed. Probably some fool had stumbled and fallen in the darkness and the rest of the platoon was running over him. His men knew better than to stop, and what better way to take out their frustration than by trampling a hapless comrade.

Bien pushed his way through the congestion. The men *had* stopped, jamming up the trail. "Spread out, you fools!"

One of his men was on his knees examining a Viet Cong with a flashlight. When the light ran across the man in the black pajamas, Bien saw he carried no pack, no rifle, nothing, and he was covered with sweat. Someone offered the guerrilla a canteen. He snatched the container and drank deeply until its owner pulled it away.

"Who is he?" demanded Bien.

"A sapper, sir. He says his squad was ambushed by Americans on the east-west trail less than an hour ago. He is the only survivor."

Bien's heart fell. The east-west trail was where the American general was! What had happened to the general?

"More water!" demanded the sapper, reaching for the canteen again.

Bien knocked the canteen aside. "You will get no more water until you have told me what happened." Bien had learned long ago never to trust a lone survivor. Lone survivors could tell their tale any way they liked, knowing there was no one to contradict them.

The soldier protested and asked for the canteen again.

Jerking out his pistol, Bien jammed the weapon into the man's mouth. "Maybe you would like to drink a little of this?"

The man gagged on the barrel and scooted back. Now the sapper recognized the man with the pistol. It was the crazy lieutenant who tortured his men with forced marches.

"Well?" asked Bien, pointing the pistol between the sapper's eyes.

Moments later, Bien was on the radio to Colonel Gzap with the bad news.

Now Gzap understood why he had lost contact with the people at the crash site. They had been wiped out by an American rescue party. But there was still hope—for some reason the Americans were moving into Cambodia, not returning to Vietnam.

Gzap stared at the map as he puffed away on a cigarette. The Americans were moving away from the border . . . toward Magic Mountain, moving deeper into Cambodia.

Why?

In the command hut no one said a word. Not even the green lieutenant.

The rescue party must have been small, considered Gzap, perhaps only a few men sent down from a helicopter. But now, these same Americans, whoever they were, were running from a squad or less of Viet Cong. And had fought their way through the sappers moving toward South Vietnam, then . . . what?

If a lurp team had done this, there was indeed a necessity for the proposal he had made to the Party that the army should establish well-trained and effective counter infiltration forces along the Ho Chi Minh Trail.

Gzap dropped his cigarette to the dirt floor and snubbed out the butt. Returning to the communications equipment, he picked up the microphone. "Bien, the Americans will attempt a liftoff from Magic Mountain. I will keep their helicopters off the mountain until you arrive. Inform me as to when you are ready to sweep up the sides of the mountain. The Americans would not dare land a helicopter under an artillery barrage, even to rescue this general. It has fallen to you to be the next hero of the Party."

* * *

The six Americans reached the base of Magic Mountain and turned south. This trail ran through Gzap's base camp, past Magic Mountain, and continued at a lazy angle toward South Vietnam. The Blue Jay Team and their wards had hustled down the trail only a few hundred yards when Magic Mountain exploded behind them. Everyone dropped to the ground and looked back. The explosions were dull thuds in the distance, but the sound carried down the trail under the jungle canopy.

"What's happening?" asked Casey.

"Artillery fire," explained Stuart. "Someone's taking Magic Mountain apart."

"But who? Why?"

Down the trail, Pike kicked something off into the jungle. "Charlie! That's who! I didn't get them all."

"No sweat," Eskew said. "We couldn't use that hill anyway. Got no radio to call in a chopper."

Everyone stood while Pike fussed and cussed and kicked more debris off the trail.

Casey turned to Stuart. "If your radio had worked we'd be on top of that mountain, wouldn't we?"

"I'd rather not think about it."

"No—I don't imagine you would."

"I'd rather be lucky than good," Lancaster said.

"Pike," Stuart said, "when you start out again cut your lead time in half."

"But Blue Jay, they'll be on top of us before I can warn you."

"Then we'll hear them coming and step off the trail. If Charlie's coming from the south, he'll be coming fast."

"You think we can just sidestep them?" asked Casey. Since crashing into the jungle everything had been so chaotic, so helter-skelter, Casey wanted to know the next thing was going to work, was something she could count on.

"The artillery proves it," Stuart said. "If there's anyone to the south of us, they will've been called up here, and on the double, to trap us on Magic Mountain. There's no reason to fight them."

"You've got that right," muttered Lancaster.

"Willie Tee, I want you behind Pike. We're going to walk and walk very fast in a tight column."

"Another good idea."

Eskew looked at the wounded man. "Lancaster, I never should have given you that morphine."

"Hey, I'm the one who was in favor of passing out."

"Move out," said Stuart, gripping Lancaster's good arm. "I have rear guard. With Charlie looking for us on Magic Mountain there shouldn't be anyone coming down the trail behind us."

"Yeah," Eskew said. "Shouldn't be."

*　　*　　*

The American command bunker in Long Bien was totally confused. The airborne unit recrossing into South Vietnam had failed to find the Blue Jay Team on the east-west trail, and the North Vietnamese were shelling Magic Mountain, several kilometers from the crash site, but in the wrong direction . . . to everyone's way of thinking. What had they missed?

"Charlie evidently thinks we'll use Magic Mountain as a landing zone," suggested Captain Manley standing at the foot of the communications console.

"But why?" asked the artillery liaison, another officer gathered there.

The officer of the day stood on the platform above them and studied the map across the room. "Charlie thinks Blue Jay will be lifted off from Magic Mountain. That's all it can mean."

"But Blue Jay's radio doesn't work," said another colonel. "There's no way he can call for a liftoff."

"Charlie doesn't know that."

"But why take Falcon deeper into Cambodia?" asked the artillery liaison. "If it were me, I'd want the hell out of there, especially if there were only two other GIs with me, and I had to bring out any wounded."

Daniels snapped his fingers. "But if you were only part of a three-man team and you were carrying wounded, you'd take the path of least resistance no matter which way Charlie pushed you." The OD glanced at the map. "Even if it meant going deeper into Cambodia. Somehow Charlie knows that's what Blue Jay's had to do. Maybe those Charlies that Blue Jay snatched Falcon from had a radio . . . ." Daniels looked at the navy captain. "Ready to take out that Charlie battery of artillery?"

"At your command, sir!" The naval captain hurried back to his desk and snatched up the phone.

"Then do it!" Daniels looked to Manley, who had also returned to his post. "Get your men ready to land on Magic Mountain. Tell them they'll have only seconds to extract Blue Jay and his team because Charlie's sure to have backup artillery standing by."

"Yes, sir!" Manley also snatched up a phone.

"Colonel Daniels!" It was the navy captain who had been told to take out the NVA artillery. "I have a forward observer who says the shelling of Magic Mountain has ceased."

"What?"

All heads turned in the naval captain's direction.

"Yes, sir. Charlie's stopped shelling Magic Mountain," repeated the navy man.

Now all heads turned back to the officer of the day.

"Charlie doesn't care if I land my men there?"

"Evidently not, sir."

A silence descended on the room, most of the soldiers staring at the huge map, specifically the area around Magic Mountain.

"Manley, suspend any additional operations." Daniels looked around the room as the men faced him. "Okay, I'm open to suggestions. Where's the Blue Jay team, and most importantly, where the hell's Falcon?"

✳   ✳   ✳

Even before the artillery barrage stopped, Lt. Bien had his platoon swarming up Magic Mountain. Minutes later, he was on the radio with the bad news.

It was not what his superior wanted to hear. Since halting the artillery fire, Gzap had been pacing back and forth across the command hut, burning up one cigarette after another. Gzap could feel the American general slipping away. Escape should be impossible, and people would testify to that—at his court-martial. He could not believe what he was hearing from the field and made Bien repeat his report from Magic Mountain.

"Sir, there is no one up here."

"What are you talking about?" screamed Gzap. "Are you sure?"

"Yes, sir. We have covered every square meter. As you know, this is not much of a mountain, more like a steep hill, and my men—"

"I know what the terrain's like. Did you see helicopters lifting off as you were coming up?"

"There were no helicopters. I can vouch for that."

"Have you questioned your men? Each and every one of them?"

"None of my men saw or heard anything, sir, and we covered all the trails as we came up. I even left men at the base of the mountain. Runners report hearing nothing, seeing nothing."

"No rifles firing?"

"No signals from my men at all."

Gzap was silent, staring at the map.

Where were the Americans? How could they have missed them? Bien was one of his best, turning down promotions, complaining any promotion would take him away from action in the field. Bien would have found the Americans if they had been there.

"It does not make sense," Bien went on. "We were not that far away—"

"Quiet!"

The command net went silent.

Bien waited. His men shifted around and looked at the holes in the mountain top. Should they be standing where artillery had so recently fallen? Maybe not every artillery battery knew they were up here. It had happened before, and each man had his own horror tale to tell. At least they could catch their breath. Canteens were taken out and passed around. Bien was in the middle of warning his men about cramping up when Gzap's voice crackled over his handset.

"Split your platoon in half. Two squads are to stay on Magic Mountain. I will send down a radio. One squad at the base, the other on the mountaintop—while you take the other two squads down the southeastern trail. And do it on the double."

"Sir?"

"Think about it, Bien. This general is the most important leader the Americans have, and the Americans would not hesitate to do whatever it takes to return him to Vietnam. If you have failed to locate him on Magic Mountain, it is because his rescue party has not yet arrived, which is unlikely because of the wounded sapper—"

"Or the party with which the general is traveling has a malfunctioning radio and there is no way they can call in a helicopter."

"That has to be the answer. If the Americans double back on the east-west trail and head for Vietnam—I have that trail covered from the other side of the border— that leaves only the southeastern trail as a means of escape, and a very good route it is indeed. The Americans know we have few troops along the river, just a few riverboats."

"They will not get away, sir."

"Make sure they do not. It will be your head."

✳   ✳   ✳

An hour later the Americans on the southeastern trail took a break. Casey asked for and received some water. She took a few careful sips, hunched down, and offered the rubber canteen to Lancaster who sat across the trail from her. From both sides of the trail came the sounds of crickets, and huddled a few yards away was the rest of the team, murmuring among themselves.

After Lancaster took a sip, Casey fastened the top back on the canteen. "I never did thank you for rescuing me."

"Looks like I didn't do such a good job." The injured man sat upright against a tree.

"You did just fine—until Charlie arrived. You even knew they were playing me for a fool."

Lancaster watched as the moon passed from behind some clouds. "We're out of the jungle. I never noticed."

"Happened about six hundred yards after we turned south."

He looked at her. "You're pretty observant for a woman."

"I'm supposed to be a reporter."

He looked skyward again. "You see those clouds—"

"Yes—it's going to rain."

Lancaster stared at her again.

"My father taught me . . . ." Casey gestured up and down the trail. "He used to do this—running around, playing soldier."

"Out here, lady, we're not playing."

138

"'Casey,' please, and you're right, it's for keeps. I had a quick course in survival this afternoon. I take it you're regular army?"

"Fuck the army! Pardon my French, but I was drafted." He glanced down the trail where Falcon was in conference with Eskew and Stuart. "I'm one of the thousands Falcon wanted over here to win this war."

"And will we?"

The sergeant snorted. "If the dad-blamed brass ever stops playing games."

"Like what?"

He glanced at the conference again. "All the brass plays CYA—cover your ass. The lieutenants, like Blue Jay, and some of the captains are okay, but once they make major, officers aren't worth a darn. Always thinking what they do will affect their careers." Lancaster paused. "What's your daddy's rank? Maybe I should've asked before blowing off."

"Almost a master sergeant when he disappeared. He's listed as missing in action."

"Sorry 'bout that. What was his MOS?"

"What? Oh, his job? Daddy was airborne." Casey looked down the trail. "Probably like Stuart."

"You sure don't know much about the army to be an army brat."

"I wasn't one long. When I was eleven my mother divorced my father for doing just this." She gestured up and down the trail. "And two of the years my parents were married, we lived with my grandmother in Chicago while my father served in Korea. My mother and sisters live in Chicago now."

"You're still mad at him, aren't you?"

"At my father? Oh, no, I don't think so. Not any more—since he's missing in action."

"Uh-huh. Maybe because he *is* missing."

Casey stared at the ground. "I guess I am, especially about his dying. He didn't have to . . . didn't have to keep on doing this. He didn't have to keep worrying my mother. He could've stopped . . . volunteering, but he didn't."

"And you're over here looking for him?"

"Oh, no," Casey said, her head coming up. "Daddy didn't disappear anywhere near here."

"That's not what I meant and you know it."

Casey swallowed and fiddled with the top of the canteen.

"I wish it wasn't going to rain."

She looked up. Lancaster was staring at the clouds.

"Well, at least it would cool us off."

"Not me, it wouldn't."

Casey put a hand to the sergeant's forehead and felt the heat. "How come you haven't passed out?"

"Morphine makes you feel like you can walk forever. But it won't last long. Even another dose. Wish it would. I'll walk 'til I drop to get out of this miserable little country. I'm sick and tired of this dad-gum place. I just want to go home. To my family." Lancaster coughed. "You think you'd like it to rain. That's something else your old man could've taught you. Rain turns the trails to mush. Charlie won't have any trouble tracking us."

Casey looked in the direction they'd just come. It certainly was dark back there. How far ahead of the enemy were they? "I hadn't thought of that."

Lancaster harrumphed. "And you never thought you'd be chased halfway across Cambodia, did you?"

"No," she said, shaking her head and smiling. "But it comes with the territory. I have a story to file." She glanced at Falcon, who was listening intently to Stuart. "And one hell of a story it's turned out to be."

Lancaster glanced at the powwow ahead of them. "It can't make them look good. Falcon being shot down and all that."

"That's tough."

"Uh-huh. Have any witnesses?"

Casey glanced down the trail. Pike was posted ahead of the conference, pulling security. "Oh, I'd say I have plenty."

"How many are civilians?"

"What are you saying, Lancaster?"

The wounded man shrugged, causing him to grimace in pain. Once he'd caught his breath, he said, "What I'm saying is, beyond the crash—and when the army reports the story, you can bet Falcon's chopper won't have gone down inside Cambodia." He smiled. "Kind of reflects on the judgment of the commanding general to crash in an area put off-limits by the president. So all you'll be able to prove is Falcon's chopper crashed, and the only reason the army'll admit that is they'll have to. Several men died in that crash—one of them a civilian. And Falcon's chopper couldn't have been shot down by a measly Viet Cong. If that's possible, what does that mean for the rest of that fancy equipment the Pentagon sends over here? A lot of taxpayers' money was spent on that equipment. No, that wouldn't do, wouldn't do at all. So right now, Long Bien's hustling to save Falcon—us, too. But you can count on another group working to protect the army's reputation. And I'm sure those folks have already been in touch with whoever owns your newspaper."

"Wire service."

"Whatever," Lancaster said with a careless wave of his good hand.

"I've gone alone on stories before. That's how I got this job."

"Not this alone. This is the biggest embarrassment to the army since MacArthur was kicked out of Korea. The army'll do anything to keep this under wraps. They can't allow Vietnam to become an embarrassment to them."

"I'll stay on them. Rag them about it. They'll have to tell what happened, if I hound them long enough."

"Well," he said with a smile, "first you have to get out of here. Alive." Lancaster stared at her. "Don't you reporters have to have some kind of credentials to be able to report from over here?"

"From the government of South Vietnam," Casey said and immediately regretted it.

"Then there's your answer," said the wounded man with a smile. "Don't report what happened out here and you'll be allowed to continue working here. And if you think you can save this story until you get home, well, the army will have the lid on so dad-blame tight . . . ."

"What about you? You could be my witness. It only takes one."

"You think I want a dishonorable discharge? I'm from

West Texas. Back there they support this war. If I help you, how do I go home? How do I ever find a decent job?" Even his father-in-law wouldn't have him in the hardware business.

"West Texas isn't the whole world. There are other places to live, to find jobs."

"Maybe to somebody who lives out of a suitcase, but I have kin back there, and where I come from, kin is awfully important."

"I have a family, too."

"You might have that mother and sisters you talked about, but you sure the devil don't have a husband. No woman who's married would be over here, and all the married men were either drafted or they're dad-blame fools for being here."

Casey couldn't help laughing. "That's what my mother said about my daddy, and more than once."

"Your mama was right. I was full of myself when I got here, but old Victor Charlie, he took the strut right out of me. Now all I want is to go home." He paused. "You'd better leave, too, Casey, or you're liable to find out something you won't like about yourself and you'll have to live with it the rest of your life."

CHAPTER
THIRTEEN

The survivors of the helicopter crash and the Blue Jay Team limped down the southeastern trail. From time to time Falcon had to be given a hand by Willie Eskew. One of the general's knees was bothering him, and it gave Casey no satisfaction that it was the same knee Falcon had injured playing tennis in Saigon.

Casey's first story from the war zone had been a scathing attack on Falcon—"General Plays While GIs Die"—and she had been chastised at the Five O'Clock Follies. One of Falcon's aides had asked, if the CIC was putting in sixteen-hour days, wasn't he allowed an hour off each day for a little recreation?

Standing her ground and returning fire, Casey had asked when the men in the field got *their* hour off? GIs deserved a break more than any general, she'd argued, since it was the grunts who were bearing the brunt of this war.

The comeback had earned Casey an "attaboy" from

Robert Sligh and a round of applause from the other reporters—drowning out the briefing officer who tried to point out that all field personnel were rotated to the rear every several months for a few days off, and that Falcon sometimes put in sixteen- to eighteen-hour days.

But out here, with Charlie on their heels, the irony bit even deeper. Ahead of her, Lancaster was practically being carried by Lt. Stuart, and it wouldn't be long before someone would have to do the same for her. Casey's legs ached, her lungs burned, and stitches had returned to both sides. If Charlie didn't kill her, the forced march would. Rain hit her in the face. She looked up and saw the moon partially hidden behind some clouds. Big, fat, juicy ones. At any moment it was going to pour again, as it had half an hour ago, making life miserable.

"Please don't rain," Casey pleaded with the sky.

Lancaster had been right. When it rained, it was hard to stay on your feet—at a time when they needed to put some distance between them and an enemy who had to be hightailing it down the trail right behind them.

Casey slipped and fell, landing on her butt. It was impossible to get any wetter, any dirtier than she was. Neither could her hair. It was a real mess, streaming down the sides of her head, dangling over her forehead in her face. Like the damn rain. Someone should've told her to have her hair cut before coming overseas.

And who would that have been? All the editors were men, most old enough to be bald. Casey pushed back her hair, hooking it behind her ears. Damn! What she wouldn't give for a rubber band. She'd have to look into having her hair trimmed when she returned to Saigon. There had to be some kind of cut that'd be shorter but still stylish, one that didn't become so yucky during the rainy season. Maybe a pageboy. Yeah, a pageboy might do it. Then again, if she had to wear her hair in that style, maybe she'd rather live with it dangling in her face.

From where she sat in the middle of the trail, Casey saw Stuart and Lancaster disappear over the next rise. There was no rear guard; she was being left behind. She struggled to her feet and slugged her way up the rise. Damn this hill! And damn the trail, too! It was muddy as hell, and adding insult to injury, uphill. Then downhill. Like now. Going downhill. That was hell on your thighs. Gil once told her when running in marathons that going downhill was—

Casey's feet slipped and she landed on her bottom again. She skidded downhill, mud gathering in the vee of her crotch, hands being nicked and scraped as she tried to stop by grabbing at the foliage beside the trail. At the bottom of the rise, Casey slid to a halt. Her shoulders sagged, her arms went limp, and she stared at the muck in her crotch.

She was finished. They'd have to go on without her. Tears ran down her face and she raised a muddy hand to wipe them away, smearing her face with filth.

Stuart appeared out of the darkness and hauled her to her feet. "Come on, girl. You can do it."

Once she was back on her feet, Casey threw off his hand. "This *woman* wants to do it on her own, if you don't mind!" She tromped down the trail, tossing her head and throwing back her hair. The bastard didn't think she could make it. She'd show him.

"And you could—if you were in shape."

She glanced over her shoulder. "What's this? A pep talk?" Damn, this guy had the same voice that had pushed her from birth to be something she could never be: a man.

"I'm not pumping you up, just saying you have the right body for hiking. Long legs for making decent time and no extra weight along for the ride. You just need more wind, and that comes only with experience."

Casey laughed as she continued walking down the trail. "Here I am out in the middle of the jungle and what's the man talking about? My body."

"We never change, do we?"

"No, and most of you like playing war, too."

"The men in my team were all drafted, Miss Blackburn."

Casey stopped and faced him, moisture running down her face, dripping off her nose. She brushed the hair out of her eyes. "Don't try to pull that on me. Men in lurp patrols volunteer for this duty. Pike and Willie Tee want to be here. Probably want to be here—with you; and you, Stuart, you had to have seen combat duty elsewhere before being given command of this team."

He only stared at her. That gave Casey time to start down the trail again.

Very quickly, Stuart caught up with her, holding her up by seizing her arm. "Miss Blackburn?"

She turned around to shrug off his hand, then saw

what lay in the palm of his hand: a rubber band. Casey nodded her thanks, pulled back her hair, and looped it with the rubber band. She started off again as Stuart tried to reason with her.

"Pike and Willie Tee think as I do: that the best way to end this war is by taking it to the enemy, wherever they might be."

Casey shook her head but didn't stop walking. "No— the best way is for you to go home."

"And let the North Vietnamese have South Vietnam."

"They have before—when the Chinese haven't had their foot on the North Vietnamese's necks. You can't stop the flow of history."

"You're well-read for a reporter."

"It wasn't all that difficult. There're only a few books, and they're all by the same guy. He predicted your defeat, too."

"I think I've improved on what Bernard Fall has to say. Do you know how many GIs are in the field fighting Charlie?"

"From the body counts the army gives me, I'd say just about everyone."

Blue Jay went silent and stayed that way.

"Okay, okay," Casey said, "that was a cheap shot, but I'm losing patience with myself in this muck. I shouldn't take it out on you. I'd guess about half the GIs are in the field."

"Wrong. Only three out of every ten."

She turned around and stopped. "Are you serious? Three out of every ten?" Casey did some quick math in her head. "Only about sixty thousand men? A hundred and forty thousand men in the rear. Doing what?"

"Support—from what they tell me."

"Nobody needs that much support. Are you sure about your numbers?"

Stuart nodded. "This army is being operated like it was in Korea or World War Two. This army has forgotten how we won our own independence. Charlie's using those same tactics against us: Indian tactics. The British used similar tactics to kick the communists out of Malaysia."

"Certainly Falcon knows about this?"

"I don't think Falcon went to West Point to hide behind trees and shoot at people. What Falcon wants, as does that whole crowd back in Long Bien, is a conventional war. A war he was taught to fight, and a war he successfully fought in World War Two and Korea."

Stuart pointed down the trail. Casey glanced ahead and saw the others moving away. She started off, walking rapidly.

"Just think," Stuart went on as he trailed along behind her, "how quickly the NVA would lose interest in coming south if we doubled the number of men in the field, and all those men were waiting, in ambush, for Charlie to come along."

"You'd still have the Army of South Vietnam sitting on their asses and letting you do all the fighting."

"Would we, Miss Blackburn? The ARVNs have seven out of ten men in the rear. The ARVNs learned that from us."

"You think the ARVNs can stand up to the NVA?"

"Don't tell me you buy into this invincible NVA rubbish. The last Asians who thought they were invincible got their asses kicked off the island of Guadalcanal by the US Marines."

"What about Korea?"

"A political war."

"And Vietnam is not?"

"It doesn't matter. The same jungle that hides the Vietnamese can hide us or the ARVNs. Besides, the NVA are nothing more than a bunch of farmers from the Red River Valley or city boys from Hanoi, not fighting men."

Casey glanced behind them. "Then why are we on the run from them?"

"Because our mission is to return Falcon to South Vietnam, not destroy the unit following us."

Casey wanted to question Stuart further about his tactics, but ahead of her everyone was slipping off the trail, disappearing into the darkness. A chill ran through her. "Charlie?" She started for the side of the trail.

Stuart took her arm and pulled her down the trail to where the others had disappeared. "Follow them in there and find a place to take off your boots and socks."

"Take off my boots and socks?"

"Yes, and be quick about it." Stuart left her, disappearing in the darkness.

Casey was left standing on the side of the trail and watching him go. The cicadas and frogs picked that moment to remind her she was stuck in the middle of a jungle. More rain dripped from trees, thumping her on the head. Funny, she hadn't noticed the jungle noises and rain while arguing with Stuart.

Eskew appeared, took Casey by the arm, and tugged her into an area where everyone sat on a log taking off their boots and socks. Everyone but Lancaster. Lancaster was out cold, lying on his back in the mushy ground.

Casey tried to go to him, but Eskew steered her over to the log. "Not now, Casey."

She sat down and followed the others' lead in taking off her boots and socks but couldn't keep her eyes off Lancaster. Wasn't there a faster way of returning to Vietnam? When she had one boot and a sock off, she asked, "Why'm I doing this? Charlie could come along and we'd have to run for it—without our boots on."

"A chance we'll have to take. As for taking off your boots and socks, mud leaves tracks, and at night our feet will look like Cambodian feet. They don't wear shoes on this side of the border, not even Ho Chi Minh sandals," said the black man, referring to the Vietnamese habit of cutting up old tires to make sandals out of them, thongs and all.

"Wait a minute, if going barefoot's so important why didn't we do it sooner?"

"Because we've come to a fork in the trail. The left leads back to the 'Nam; the right leads to a village along the river. Blue Jay's decided to use the boats from that village to take us back to South Vietnam."

Stuart had decided, had he? Well, she was sick and tired of Stuart making all the decisions. "We're moving away from Vietnam. What's that do for Lancaster?"

"Actually we'll be paralleling the border, but don't worry about it. The river runs into 'Nam, and we'll be safer in boats. Charlie didn't find us up north so he'll be sending his people down here." Eskew gestured at the unconscious Lancaster with one of his green canvas-topped jungle boots. "And Charlie won't slow down for wounded either. He can leave them behind."

Casey remembered slugging her way down the trail, slipping and sliding and falling on her butt. Anything was better than that. Maybe Stuart was right. Maybe.

Then Stuart was there, appearing out of the darkness without making a sound. But who could've heard him with all this noise: the cicadas, the frogs, and the rain dripping from the trees, hitting huge leaves.

Falcon stood up, using the log to steady himself. "I'll help you mark the trail."

Casey saw the general still had on his boots.

"Mark the trail?" she asked Stuart.

"A couple of us have to walk up and down the left fork a hundred yards or so, leaving a trail for Charlie to follow. It'll buy time for the others to reach the boats. We'll catch up with them at the river."

Casey almost laughed. "Do you really think that'll work? That has to be one of the oldest tricks . . . ." She realized everyone was staring at her.

"You had another idea, Miss Blackburn?"

"No—no. I just didn't think . . . ."

Stuart turned to Falcon. "Sorry, sir, but I'm not taking anyone who's injured, and you're having trouble with that knee."

"I'll do it," Casey heard herself say.

They all turned and stared at her.

"This isn't your responsibility, Casey."

The general's objection went beyond her not being a soldier. Casey's father had disappeared after volunteering for a rescue mission. It was in the letter Falcon had written her mother, a note of condolence to the ex-wife of a twenty-three-year veteran.

Casey wrung out a sock, then had to twist it around to get it back on her foot. "Lancaster has to be carried. That leaves only me." She looked at Stuart, but the tall man just stared at her.

"Out of the question," Falcon said, "You're a civilian."

Casey pulled on her other sock. "No, sir. Out here I don't think there are any civilians."

✳   ✳   ✳

Officer of the day Daniels was directing his airborne unit when Falcon's executive officer, or second in command, pushed his way through the double doors of the command bunker. The executive officer was a bull of a man, built like the tanks he longed to command. Instead, he was in charge of the Americans' Pacification Program, a command he didn't particularly enjoy because he had to stand up in front of his peers and vow that pacification was the solution to America's problems in Vietnam—if you weren't going to let him invade North Vietnam.

The executive officer was a tank man in a war where tanks were useless, maybe obsolete. Worse, the exec knew it, and more than one soldier had heard him joke about what progress he could make if the rain, not Charlie, would call a cease-fire.

The executive officer was the opposite of the man under whom he served. Where Falcon was spartan and remote, the exec was overweight, smoked cigars, and joked with his men. He was a soldier's soldier who didn't take himself seriously unless he was taking care of business, and at the moment, he was dead serious. He was about to do something that would bring him and other men in this room up on charges at general court martial if the press learned what they were up to.

"Ready, Daniels?" asked the exec as he mounted the communications platform with the OD.

"Yes, sir. Ready and raring."

"Then have at it."

"Yes, sir!"

Daniels turned to the men in the command bunker. Each one knew his assignment, but everyone had been waiting for someone to take responsibility.

"Go!" ordered Daniels.

On the OD's command, the navy began bombarding Colonel Gzap's base camp. The navy had promised that their guns wouldn't halt firing until Falcon reappeared on this side of the border or they ran out of ammunition. And they guaranteed they wouldn't run out of ammunition. At the same time, B-52 bombers were diverted from their targets in North Vietnam to a single, more narrow target: the Ho Chi Minh Trail. The air force's responsibility was to discourage the NVA from moving Falcon to Hanoi if he'd fallen into their hands. Simultaneously, an airborne battalion would land on Magic Mountain.

The plan was for one company to dig in and hold the

mountaintop while other companies swarmed down its sides, fanning out on the north-south, southeast, and east-west trails. Each time they came to a fork, units would break off until the entire network had been completely searched. The Americans would work with loudspeakers and lights to alert the Blue Jay Team that there were friendlies in the area, and more than one soldier had reservations about breaking the rules of night combat. But if Charlie heard the Americans coming and decided to stand and fight, as the NVA often did, so be it. After the frustrations of the past few hours, the Americans were spoiling for a fight.

CHAPTER
FOURTEEN

After making their second walk backwards, they had returned to the split in the trail when someone came jogging toward them. Casey tried to bolt into the jungle, but Stuart grabbed her.

"No! They'll hear you." He pulled her down behind a bush at the fork in the trail.

Casey was hardly on the ground before Charlie's point man arrived. The soldier stopped and looked from one trail to the other, undecided as to which way to go. This Charlie, who happened to be wearing a radio on his back, stopped in front of the bush Casey and Stuart were hiding behind.

One by one a ragged line of soldiers drifted into sight—more than a squad, maybe a platoon—gathering along the trail in front of the Americans. Soldiers bent over, rifles across their knees, as they tried to catch their breath. None wore the black pajamas of the Viet Cong. Instead they wore the dull green uniform of North Vietnamese regulars—the real tough bastards, as Willie Tee had said. And if any of these really tough bastards cared to look, how could he miss seeing Casey huddled behind the bush? She held her breath.

The point man shouted down the column, and a couple of soldiers broke off and jogged down the trail toward the Cambodian village. Then the point man walked down the southeastern trail, examining the ground with his light. His men followed him, taking long pulls from their canteens. A command from the man with the radio on his back and the canteens were put away. One soldier was so intimidated he even spit out his water, spraying the bush Casey and Stuart hid behind.

Casey trembled, and as she crouched behind this bush, her mother's complaint about her father came into sharp focus. How could any woman sit at home and wait for some fool who enjoyed this? An indictment, not only of her father, but of the man beside her.

When Casey looked into Stuart's eyes she saw no fear but a wild excitement. The lieutenant was enjoying the pursuit as much as the Vietnamese were enjoying the chase. This was a game to them, a game authorized by governments and played to the death. And if Stuart died while playing out his role, what would be his last thoughts? What had been her father's last thoughts? Sadness? Remorse? Hardly. More likely surprise. Surprise that the game had finally turned against him.

One of the soldiers moved to the other side of the trail and unbuttoned his pants to relieve himself.

My God! If he'd chosen this side . . . Casey had an overwhelming urge to stand up and let everyone know where she was. To scream her head off. To bring the game to an end. To do something, anything to relieve the tension.

Stuart was now rubbing her shoulders, trying to calm her. He must think she was a total idiot—a complete fool! How many GIs had this lieutenant had to comfort while waiting in ambush?

None, dammit, none! Tears ran down her cheeks, burning her skin. She was *sooo* embarrassed.

The NVA soldiers who had been sent down the trail toward the Cambodian village returned, shouting what they'd found. The soldier with the radio on his back listened to what they had to say. He held one of Lancaster's bloody bandages in his hand. More of Stuart's charade, casually tossing the bandage to the side of the trail, saying it was icing on the cake. But would it work?

It just had to work.

Stuart tightened his grip on her, and Casey buried her face into his chest. Had the fools actually swallowed the bait? Their stupid, silly bait? She couldn't look. This dumb idea wouldn't work, she'd be recaptured, and before she could report—

The North Vietnamese formed up in a loose column and ran off down the trail toward South Vietnam. Casey leaned into Stuart and sobbed. It was a moment before she recovered, and when she did, she was overcome with shame. She tried to sit up, but Stuart held her in place, hand against her back.

One of the soldiers returning from the village who'd apparently gone farther than the others, cut across behind them in an effort to catch up with his unit. He tripped over Casey's foot and went down. Stuart fell on the man, and when she dared look, she saw the lieutenant on top of the Vietnamese, one hand over the man's mouth, the other holding a knife! Now where'd that come from?

The knife flashed up and down in the moonlight . . . once . . . twice . . . three times before the Vietnamese stopped wiggling and lay still. Stopped fighting for his life—that's what he'd done. Stopped fighting for his life like anyone with any sense would've done. Casey continued to tremble and wonder what in God's name she was doing here?

Stuart wiped the blade on the man's uniform and turned to her, a bloody finger at his lips. "Shhh!"

But Casey couldn't be still. The ground shook. No, it wasn't the ground, it was her. She was shaking uncontrollably. Casey threw herself into Stuart's arms and sobbed. He held her tightly and stroked her head. Now the tears were really pouring.

"I—I'm so ashamed . . . ."

"You have every right to be frightened. Those men would've killed you, right after you told them where to find Falcon."

"But I thought . . . I'd perform better . . . ."

Stuart pushed her back where he could see her, but Casey couldn't meet his eyes.

"You're expecting too much of yourself. You weren't trained for this." For the first time, Stuart smiled. "Even I wasn't trained to survive helicopter crashes."

Casey looked at his shoulders and remembered how good it felt to be in his arms. The man had shoulders a girl could find a home in, could hide from the world that was swirling around her, out of control. She wanted to return to those shoulders, to be held by those arms.

Stuart jerked Casey to her feet, and she felt the same hollowness in her chest she'd always felt whenever her father had gone overseas. On those occasions, you could do nothing, say nothing, only cry your eyes out. The future was set in stone.

Stuart started toward the Cambodian village. "Come on. That trail won't fool them long."

Casey stood there, aching for this man's arms, but he was gone, disappearing in the darkness. Her father was gone, too, having disappeared in a similar darkness. She was alone in the jungle of Southeast Asia.

She looked around. Did she really think she could strike a blow against her country's war effort or was she simply searching for her father—as Lancaster had said? Or was she searching for something else? Something she might not recognize even if she found it?

Casey glanced at the dead man at her feet. The Vietnamese lay on his back, open-eyed, as if staring at the moon. She shivered in the humid night air, then started off after Stuart. No time for feeling sorry for herself as she'd been able to do whenever her father left home. No. And if she kept her wits about her, her future in this jungle of Southeast Asia might not be set in stone.

Minutes later, Casey saw the lights of the village, and when she arrived, she saw Stuart and Willie Tee surrounded by a group of little brown men. These had to be the Cambodians, but Casey couldn't see any difference between them and the South Vietnamese. Maybe a little bit shorter, a bit stockier.

The village consisted of two rows of thatched huts, all on stilts, one row facing the other. Torches burned at strategically placed spots, and at every door, little brown children stared at Casey as she strolled through their village. Casey brushed back her hair, smiled, and waved. Some of the children disappeared inside their huts, but others edged down the ramps toward her.

Pigs, slumbering in puddles under the ramps, stirred and snorted, then went back to sleep. From the darkness came quacking and clucking. In the center of the village, the men chattered among themselves, the deeper voices of the Americans blocking out the higher-pitched sounds of the Cambodians.

Casey stopped at a ramp, stooped down, and extended a hand. A little boy looked at her, then glanced toward the mouth of the hut. A woman spoke sharply from the darkness, and the boy ran up the ramp, back inside the hut. Behind Casey, a little girl had edged down a ramp across the way. The child, appearing to be eight or nine, slipped up and touched her hair.

Casey turned around, took the girl's hand, and looked in her eyes—the more modest place to look. The girl had black hair and a stocky, lightly tanned body, but wore no clothing, nothing at all. Casey smiled, but the girl had eyes only for Casey's hair. She ran the golden strands through her fingers, mud-streaked as they were, never taking her eyes off that hair.

Seeing no harm being done to their friend, other children came down ramps and surrounded Casey, touching and pulling at her hair. Casey smiled and took their hands, but they pulled away, preferring to touch her hair. Well, blondes were scarce this—

There was a shout from behind her.

Charlie?

Casey leaped to her feet as the children scattered.

Ouch! Some of those little hands hadn't turned loose quickly enough.

The children raced up their ramps and disappeared inside their huts, not because Charlie was on his way, but because Stuart stood over their fallen chief. The elderly man lay on his back in the circle of Cambodians that surrounded the two Americans. He slowly got to his hands and knees, then stood up, looked Stuart in the eye, and shook his head. When he did, Stuart grabbed the old man's shirt, lifting him off the ground.

Could this be the same man who'd comforted her only moments ago in the thicket? If the Cambodians didn't want to share their boats, she and the others could walk back to Vietnam. The important thing was they'd thrown Charlie off their trail. Casey attempted to break through the Cambodians, but Eskew grabbed her arm.

"No, Casey! You can't!"

She turned on the black man, eyes flashing. "You just watch me!"

"Don't interfere in this. You're only a woman."

Casey gaped at him. It was the most outrageous thing she'd ever heard!

"No matter what happens, nothing could be worse than for that old man to be defended by a woman. Any woman. You'd only—"

At the sound of the slap, they looked at Stuart and the chief. The elderly man was in the air, being held up by his shirt, eye level to the taller American. The two men glared at each other. Blood dribbled out of the corner of the chief's mouth. The elderly man said nothing but shook his head again.

One of the Cambodians—none of them had any weapons as far as Casey could see—stepped forward, challenging Stuart. Eskew let go of Casey and swung his rifle around. The Cambodian saw the rifle but didn't back off until ordered to do so by his chief. Casey started for the old man and caught the barrel of Eskew's rifle across her stomach. She gasped and sunk to her knees.

Looking up, she said, "You'd shoot me, wouldn't you?"

"No, ma'am, but I won't let you interfere, either."

Stuart put down the elderly man, and with one motion turned him around, shoving his arm up behind his back. Then, by torch light, he marched the chief toward the river: an insurance policy for the boats they were about to steal.

Casey felt sick. The kidnapping of the chief greatly improved her chances of returning to Vietnam. With acid in her voice, she asked, "Can we go now?"

"Yes, ma'am," said Eskew, "but no funny business."

Casey opened her mouth to chastise him but remembered how she'd tested the patience of the Viet Cong squad leader. Her face still ached from those blows. Why couldn't she learn to keep her mouth shut? At least until she was back in Saigon.

She stepped off in the direction of the river. Back in Saigon she could have her way with these men and their precious self-images. Self-images these men wouldn't like tarnished. She'd dip their names in shit in every paper that subscribed to her wire service.

Falcon and Pike were already in the boats, none of them able to meet her eyes. Casey understood the feeling. She felt worse now than when she'd puked her guts out along the trail.

Eskew pointed to the second boat, an oversized dugout like the first. "In there," he said.

Casey tossed her head and stepped in behind Falcon. Just as well they didn't put her in the same boat with Blue Jay. No telling what she might do, even to the detriment of the damn mission!

Once she was seated, a sling rope, about six feet long and usually attached to the lurp's web gear by a snap link, was quickly fastened to her belt by Eskew, and another from Falcon's belt to her belt as he was seated forward of her in the wooden craft. Ahead of them, Stuart shoved the chief into the lead boat, stepped in himself, knelt down, and pushed off with a paddle.

Casey noticed he did not attach a sling rope to the chief, but simply guided the boat into the middle of the river as Pike dug in with a paddle at the bow. The current, intense from the rainy season runoff, sped the boat downstream, and soon Casey's boat followed in their wake. Along the shoreline, Cambodians appeared out of the darkness but made no move to stop them.

How could they? We have their chief. This was horrible. The war in Vietnam had spilled over into Cambodia. Where would it end—especially with an army full of James Stuarts, men dedicated to only one thing: the accomplishment of the damn mission, no matter the cost in human suffering?

Pike's voice floated back from the lead boat. "Home free!"

"Shut up, Pike!" ordered Stuart.

A minute later there was a loud splash, and when Casey's boat reached that spot, she saw the chief sputtering to the surface. Before he disappeared behind her, she saw him take a few clumsy strokes toward shore.

Would he make it or would he drown? Or suffer a heart attack attempting to reach the shore? Casey turned around and stared at Falcon's back. It was one thing to steal a man's boats, quite another to be a party to murder. God, but she hoped this was going to be a short trip home. She had some business to tend to. She had a score to settle with this Blue Jay Team.

Minutes later, as Casey shifted around trying to find a comfortable position on the hard bottom of the boat, she heard shouts from up ahead.

"What the hell?" said someone.

"Look out!" shouted Stuart.

In the darkness she saw nothing but felt the boat slow down, even though Falcon and Eskew dug their paddles into the water. Casey grabbed both sides of the boat, but that didn't help. They slammed into something she couldn't see, and the force of the collision ripped her hands off the sides of the boat, pitching her into the river.

CHAPTER
FIFTEEN

Robert Sligh returned to the tailor's hut but only after a thorough check of all the whorehouses and bars around Long Bien. He had found few GIs, and those GIs he did find had been there since early morning. Standing across the road from the compound entrance, Sligh watched GIs returning to the compound. Those inside were not allowed out. Sligh himself was refused entry—twice!—even after demanding to speak to the CIC or his exec. Dammit! There *was* something going on. Had the Americans finally invaded the North? Or struck at their sanctuaries in Cambodia? Either story could make a man's reputation.

When Sligh reapproached the tailor's hut it was well after nightfall. He saw another pedicab parked at the door and noticed that the space surrounding the huts was free of all children. This made his driver nervous. The pedicab stopped and the reporter was told to walk the last few meters. The tailor met him at the door.

"Take the cab, Mr. Sligh. Someone will contact you." The Vietnamese dropped the poncho liner that served as his door, leaving Sligh standing in the dark.

Sligh could see the muffled lights of the Long Bien compound across the street. He stared at the cab, then looked up and down the dirt road. Occasionally a jeep filled with MPs drove by, but otherwise the road was empty in both directions.

The driver of the pedicab parked at the door sat with head slumped on his chest, feet on the pedals, hands across his lap. For all Sligh knew, the man could be asleep. Or an assassin. Sligh snorted. Well, that was what they paid him the big bucks for. He climbed aboard.

When he took a seat, the cab made a one-hundred-and-eighty-degree turn, throwing the reporter to one side. Sligh grabbed the wire handles on each side and hung on as the pedicab made several other quick maneuvers through the village, not all of them on the road. At one point a young Vietnamese ran out of a hut and leaped into the moving cab beside Sligh. The Vietnamese wore civilian clothing and carried a small satchel.

After taking a seat, he shook hands with the reporter. "Good to meet you, Mr. Sligh. I have read many of the stories you have written about this war that is destroying my country. What can I do for you?"

"I need to get inside the American compound and I need to do it tonight."

"May I ask why?"

"There's a story in there and I want to report it."

"And what is this story?"

"I'd rather not say."

"Do you have any idea what is happening inside your countrymen's compound, Mr. Sligh?"

"No," he said, shaking his head, "I really don't."

The Vietnamese smiled. "Who told you about this story?"

He told the Vietnamese about his American source.

"Well," said the young man, leaning back, "it would appear there is more than one GI who wishes this war would come to an end. Mr. Sligh, the reason I was sent to contact you is because you have printed most of the stories that make sense about this war." He regarded the reporter. "If I gave you the biggest story of your career, could you have it published?"

Sligh couldn't help but laugh. All sources were the same. They all had the biggest story of his career. Didn't he wish they did? "Friend, the big ones don't need any help getting published. It's only when a big story dribbles in and you have to prove it, point by point, that it takes so long to make it into print."

"Then you will have no trouble printing this story. I can give you the facts, and I can give them to you to-night." The Vietnamese tapped the satchel in his lap. "You have not been allowed inside your countrymen's compound because no one wants you, or any other member of the press, to learn that your country has invaded Cambodia, a neutral country in this war."

So it had finally happened, thought Sligh. For months the CIC had wanted to strike at the sanctuaries frustrating his war effort. Now it seemed the American president had given the CIC the go-ahead.

"Where's the invasion point?"

"Magic Mountain."

"Magic Mountain?" There wasn't anything to that damn hill but its preposterous name, one of many tales told about this godforsaken country. The story was that during a visit to the Imperial City of Hue, at a time when the Vietnamese occupied Cambodia, a Cambodian princess had become involved in some court intrigue. The princess was murdered and her body was never returned to her village. These days, Cambodians saw the princess on the mountaintop, especially during the rainy season. More likely fog, thought Sligh.

The Viet Cong pulled a map from his satchel. "As you know, this mountain is sacred to all Cambodians, but that did not bother your countrymen. Every night American soldiers set up ambushes in graveyards all over my country, a country where people revere their ancestors." The Vietnamese ran his finger along the trails running north, southeast, and east from the base of Magic Mountain. "Even as you and I speak, American soldiers are marching down these trails searching for my comrades." He illuminated his work with a penlight as the pedicab moved though the darkness of the Vietnamese evening. Pointing to a spot on the map, he said, "This particular camp houses several hospitals. They might strike there next."

Sligh sighed. These people took so damn long to tell you something. In that regard they weren't much different from the army. He tapped the map. "This was the only invasion point?"

"As far as we know."

"Come on now, there have to be others. The army

has too many men, and too many ideas how to use those men, to invade at only one spot."

"Not necessarily. This could be a test to see what your government can get away with. The bombing of the North began in steps, if you remember."

"Got anything to back it up?"

The Vietnamese took a cassette recorder from his satchel. "You speak my language?"

Sligh nodded.

"This came in only minutes ago."

The tape was of Colonel Gzap reporting the shelling of his base camp and of American soldiers sweeping down the sides of Magic Mountain. Americans were also pouring across the border on the east-west trail. An explosion cut off the sound, then there was only the hiss of the tape.

Sligh touched Magic Mountain and the Vietnamese-Cambodian border on the map. "They're here and here?"

"Yes, Mr. Sligh."

"And moving in this direction?" The reporter put his fingers on the two locations—Magic Mountain and the border—and drew the fingers together across the east-west trail. "It looks like a pincer movement, like they're trying to catch somebody." Sligh looked up. "What have you got there? Ho Chi Minh's summer home?"

The Vietnamese laughed. "Hardly, Mr. Sligh."

"Then what's going on?"

"Why, your country is invading a neutral country."

"Uh-huh." Sligh tapped the recorder. "How do I know this wasn't cooked up?" Before the conversation could continue, he had to explain what "cooked up" meant.

"There is no way for you to know. But tell me, why is it you cannot get inside your countrymen's compound? Usually they will allow you to interview anyone you wish, anytime you want."

Sligh didn't have an answer. As shortsighted as the CIC was, the man prided himself on having someone available to answer reporters' questions, even if the reporter didn't think much of the answers.

"You have requested an audience with the commanding general. Is this not true?"

Sligh nodded.

"And he would not see you."

Sligh shook his head.

The Vietnamese gestured in the direction of the Long Bien compound. "By this time of day, the CIC is usually in Long Bien, reviewing the daily body count. The daily body count is very important to your secretary of defense. Is that not true?"

"What's your point?" asked Sligh.

"The commanding general has been seen across the border directing this invasion."

"Maybe . . . ."

"Mr. Sligh, I thought you were interested in gaining access to your countrymen's compound?"

The reporter leaned back as the pedicab wove its way through the village. "I am, buddy boy, but people who file this kind of story can't afford to stumble or we won't be filing many more. How were you going to get me inside—so I can ask my questions?"

"We have this tunnel—"

Sligh bolted upright. "I'm in!"

CHAPTER
SIXTEEN

Casey surfaced, spitting water and gasping for breath. She flailed around, found a rope, and grabbed hold as the river shoved her against it. She wiped hair out of her eyes and looked around. Both boats were upside down and against a rope. More horizontal strands pressed against her feet, legs, and shoulder. Torches burned on the far side of the river, illuminating a line of men yelling and gesturing for the Americans to come ashore.

The Cambodians had gotten downstream ahead of them!

When she'd thought the chief was resisting, he'd been stalling. His men had gone ahead of them, strung a rope across the river, and waited for them to fall into their trap.

Damn! And just when she was beginning to believe they *were* home free. They weren't anywhere close.

Eskew broke the surface, shaking off water. "It's a

net, not a rope. We can't go under or around it." He glanced toward shore. "And I don't think those guys are going to give us a chance to climb over."

In answer to his comment, shots were fired from shore and water kicked up in Casey's face. She yelped and quickly ran her hand down the rope, then left and right. Eskew was right. It was a net. They were trapped!

More shots kicked up more water.

"We're sitting ducks out here!" hollered Pike.

"Come on," said Eskew with resignation in his voice. "Let's go ashore." He unhooked the ropes tying him to Casey and started hand over hand toward the riverbank.

It was all Casey could do to follow. The emotional roller coaster she'd been riding since crashing into the jungle had just taken its worst dip. Numbly, she put one hand over the other and followed Eskew along the top of the net. It was slow going. Her clothing clung to her, and her boots were waterlogged—dead weights at the end of each leg. One by one the other members of the party bunched up behind her.

Falcon said, "Just put one hand in front of the other and you'll make it."

"You say," she snapped as she struggled against a river forcing her into the entangling net.

"You're a fine young lady, Casey. Your father would've been proud of you."

"What's this? Injecting personalities into war?"

Casey really wished she hadn't said that, but she was so tired. Her body ached. Nothing was working out. Nothing at all.

"And you've got K.C.'s tongue," finished Falcon. "That's why your father never made master sergeant."

Ahead of them, Eskew crawled ashore. His rifle was snatched off his back where it had been slung. He was stripped of his rucksack, and he was shoved toward a ridge where two Cambodians waited, rifles at the ready. Casey had seen no rifles back in the village, and for good reason. No rifles meant there would be no shooting near the village so their women and children would be safe. Once the Americans were downstream, away from their families, the Cambodians could trap them, as they had done now.

A moment later, Casey struggled ashore, where she was shouted at, pulled from the water, and propelled toward the ridge. Eskew grabbed her as she stumbled over, collapsing into his arms. He turned her away from the guards who were openly gaping at her.

Eskew pulled off his boonie hat and shoved it in her hands. "Put this on. Now!" He moved to stand between her and the guards.

Casey stared at the hat, then used her weary arms to cram her hair up and under it. It was *sooo* hard to make her arms respond. All they wanted to do was hang limply at her sides. When would this ever end? Seeing the light from the torches glint off the barrels of the guards' rifles, Casey realized it might be over here and now, in the backwaters of some Third World country. Not exactly what she had in mind when she'd signed up for her first journalism courses.

One by one the rest of the team were pulled from the river, stripped of their gear, and shoved toward the ridge, where they stood dripping water and huddling around her. The last man out was Stuart, bringing Lancaster along.

"Oh, no!" Lost in her world of self-pity, Casey had forgotten about the injured man. She wanted to go to Lancaster, to comfort him, but when she stepped forward, Falcon held her back.

"It's best you stay here."

A glance at how carelessly their guards handled their rifles told her Falcon was right. Any sudden movement endangered not only Lancaster but the whole team.

Dammit! When was she going to get it through her head that she was a member of this team? Not a very effective member but still a member, someone others might count on. Count on for what, she didn't know, but to forget they had wounded . . . how could she?

"Lancaster's out of it," said Pike, as the wounded man was dumped on the riverbank.

"He's lost too much blood."

"You give him the serum albumin?"

"Back at the village," Eskew said. "Lancaster needs a transfusion, not a blood expander."

As they watched, Lancaster was pulled to his feet and expected to stand. When they let him go, the injured man crumpled to the ground. One of the Cambodians kicked him.

"Assholes!" muttered Pike.

Stuart stumbled over and pushed away the Cambodians who had kicked Lancaster. For his trouble, he was thumped across the back with a rifle. Luckily, the blow landed on the radio. Under the blow, and the weight of his rucksack and radio, the lieutenant stumbled forward, then went to his hands and knees. When he looked up, he found several rifles and pistols in his face. He slowly got to his feet.

Casey said, "They're paying him back for throwing their chief in the river."

Eskew stared at her. "What you talking about, woman? Blue Jay had to slap that old man around so Charlie wouldn't kill him for letting us have his boats."

Casey looked at Stuart, who was being stripped of his rucksack, radio, and rifle. How could she have been so wrong about this man? Her father would have said, "You're thinking like a civilian." And she would've snapped back, "Yes, thank God." But out here in this jungle, pursued by Charlie and now captured by these Cambodians, thinking like a civilian just might get her killed.

The Cambodians had returned to kicking the un-conscious man. Lancaster moaned and rolled over, but didn't get to his feet. He didn't even open his eyes.

This was how they treated someone who'd come down through the jungle to rescue her? Someone who'd run interference through that sapper squad? It wasn't right, not right at all. But when Casey tried to go to Lancaster, Falcon and Eskew held her back again.

"Stay here! Don't let them see you."

One of the Cambodians picked up Stuart's radio, turned to the ridge, and held the instrument overhead. On the ridge was a man with gray hair, arms folded across his chest. Torches flanked him. He motioned for the radio to be brought up to him.

Clunk!

Everyone looked back to the men guarding Lancaster. Stuart had come up from behind them as the two guards watched the radio being shown off. He had grabbed the two shorter men—one under each arm— and rammed their heads together.

Clunk!

Blue Jay did it again, then dropped the Cambodians to the ground. The man holding the radio backed away, clutching his new possession. Another Cambodian ran up behind Blue Jay and clubbed him across the back. He wasn't tall enough to reach the American's head with the blow—but he could now as Stuart sunk to his knees.

"No!" screamed Casey as she burst through Eskew and Falcon. Her boonie hat flew off as she raced across the riverbank.

The guards' rifles followed her, then swung around on Eskew, Pike, and Falcon when they, too, stepped forward. The guards motioned the Americans back under the ridge. The man who was about to club Blue Jay with his rifle butt looked up and saw Casey racing toward him. The Cambodian had time only to twist his rifle around and get off one quick shot before she was on him, knocking him to the ground. The shot went wild, the rifle flew out of the man's hands, and he ended up flat on his back. Casey straddled him, and when the Cambodian tried to shove her off, she braced herself using her knees.

She'd had enough of this! Ever since falling into this damn jungle people had been pushing her around, telling her what to do, chasing her here and there. Now it was her turn! When her nails ripped into the Cambodian's face, he screeched in pain and grabbed her wrists. He twisted back and forth, bucking up and down, but couldn't throw off a woman who weighed about the same as he did.

Hands slipped under Casey's arms and she was pulled to her feet. Her victim scooted back, wiping blood from his face and catching his breath. When he saw it had been a woman who had attacked him, he leaped to his feet and came at her with a maniacal grin. Before he could reach her, Casey remembered what she'd failed to do when slapped silly by the Viet Cong squad leader. She kicked the man in the groin. The Cambodian tried to scream, but could only croak. He slid to his knees holding his crotch with both hands, then fell to one side, groaning.

There was a shout, and hands whirled Casey around so the man on the ridge could see her. A light was thrust in her face. The torch was so bright, so hot, Casey closed her eyes and turned away. One of the Cambodians grabbed her by the hair and turned her to face the ridge. Casey yipped in pain.

A murmur ran through the crowd. The Cambodians closed in, giving her the once-over. It made Casey wish she'd remained hidden behind the other members of the team. Hell, truth be known, she'd rather be back in Saigon. Matter of fact, stateside wouldn't be so bad right about now. Casey felt hands in her hair, fingering it. This was the stateside psycho all over again. In spades.

Her guards loosened their grips to feel her hair. When they did, she spun away. "Get your hands off me!"

They backed away, but more to make way for the man striding down from the ridge. Casey ignored the older man. Seeing that Stuart was okay—he was sitting up and rubbing the back of his head—she went to one knee beside Lancaster.

Because the torch burned in her vision as if she'd looked into the sun, Casey had to feel around for the buttons of Lancaster's fatigue blouse. She also had to pull her hair back behind her ears. The rubber band Stuart had given her was gone. She fought with the wet holes and buttons, opened Lancaster's shirt, and peeled it back so she could find the patch.

The wadding was soaked with blood and water. Casey untied the soggy thing and wrung it out, then replaced it over the hole in the unconscious man's side. At the rate Lancaster was losing blood, he'd be dead before they recrossed the border. They had to . . . .

Someone was in her light. Casey looked up and scowled. It was the old man from the ridge. He spoke to her and Casey ignored him.

"He wants you to stand up so he can get a better look at you," said Stuart, already on his feet.

"Once I'm finished here."

Casey repositioned the patch, and Lancaster didn't make a sound. He was out of it. They had to get Lancaster to a hospital, call in a chopper, locate a radio—one that worked. Do something.

"He says he'll put a hole in you like the ones in Lancaster if you don't stand up."

"Tell him to go ahead."

When Stuart translated her reply, Casey heard a pistol slide out of its holster and the hammer cocked. That didn't stop her. She'd had her fill of this jungle and its bully boys.

Blue Jay grabbed her, pulling her to her feet. "Don't mess with these people, Casey. Bandits are the law when Charlie's not around, and if you haven't noticed, Charlie's not around."

"Bandits?" And for the first time Casey noticed the ragtag nature of these men. Most wore ill-matching clothes, and their hands held a variety of weapons: rifles, pistols, or machetes. Some even carried clubs. Bandoliers, half-full, ran across the chests of a few.

"Yes, bandits, and bandits can kill you just as quickly as Charlie, maybe quicker."

The old man holstered his pistol, reached out, and took some of Casey's hair in his hand. His eyes widened as he examined it. She backed away, pulling her hair out of his grasp. She didn't want those leathery hands anywhere near her body.

There was a quick question from the Cambodian, then a longer explanation from Stuart.

"What's going on?" she asked.

"He wants to know what we're doing here. I told him about the helicopter crash, that Charlie's on our tail, and how pleased our government would be if he helped us cross the border. I said for the man who did that, there would be plenty of clothing, equipment, and medicine."

"But no guns."

The bandit leader spoke again.

"That's what he's asking for now." Stuart pointed at his team's rifles, then held out his hands, palms up.

The bandit gestured at the other members of the team standing under the ridge and said something. Stuart shook his head. The Cambodian spoke sharply, and the guards' rifles came up at the Americans under the ridge. Eskew and Pike moved to stand in front of Falcon. Jerking a thumb at his chest, Stuart said something.

Casey grabbed his arm. "What's going on?"

He threw her hand off. "Stay out of this! I can't convince him I'm serious with a woman hanging on me."

Casey backed off, her hands becoming fists she'd very much like to use on either man. Convince this bandit they were serious? Shit! The mood she was in, let her give it a go. She'd convince the bastards to carry them to Saigon. On their backs.

The leader gestured at Casey. This resulted in another exchange that disintegrated into an argument between the bandit leader and Blue Jay. Stuart shook his head. The bandit jerked out his pistol and pointed it at the lieutenant. Again the American shook his head.

Casey couldn't help stepping back. God, but Stuart was a cool one, and it made her wonder if this was how her father had died? With grace under pressure? What a waste. Give the bastards what they want. What could a few more guns matter in this damn war?

The bandit leader spoke again and the pistol was shifted from Stuart to the unconscious Lancaster. The bandit leader pulled back on the hammer again.

Casey reached for Stuart again. "For God's sake, give them what they want!"

Stuart turned on her, his eyes like black ice. "They want *you!* You're to stay here until I return with what we've bargained for."

Casey opened her mouth but found she couldn't speak. She was choking on her own fear.

Stuart nodded to the Cambodian.

The bandit grinned, put away his pistol, and appraised his hostage.

"What'd you do?" Casey's voice returned with vigor. "You didn't agree, did you?"

"I did."

Casey couldn't get her breath. The torches blurred her vision and the world swam around her. Still, she didn't have to be able to see to know what these nasty little devils had in mind if she *was* left behind. First it would be their leader; then she'd be passed around until there was nothing left, nothing anyone would recognize as Casey Blackburn. Stuart had finally found a way to keep her from reporting what she'd seen out here. How could she expose these men without being exposed herself? Or continue reporting from Vietnam with people snickering behind her back.

Casey swung at Stuart with all her might, a well-telegraphed blow he didn't block or duck. He just stood there and took it. Right across the face.

"You can't . . . you can't consider leaving me out here . . . ." She looked around, her voice breaking. "With . . . with these animals."

"I'll be back by morning."

Tears started down her cheeks. "I—I won't be here when you return." Casey couldn't stop the tears and found she didn't care to. "It—it won't be me you'll find. Can't—can't you see that?"

"I'll be back by morning," said Stuart, as if it were the answer to all her problems.

"Then leave someone with me. Willie Tee or Pike. Please!"

Stuart glanced at the bandit leader who was watching their conversation very closely. "He won't allow it."

"Did you even ask?"

"Of course."

"I don't believe you."

But the lieutenant had turned to speak to his men. The Americans under the ridge looked at their guards, who glanced at their leader. The bandit leader nodded, and the guards motioned the Americans back to the river. None of the three men looked at Casey as they returned to their boats, and it had nothing to do with the fact that they had to take the unconscious Lancaster along.

"Please don't do this," pleaded Casey. "You don't have to do this."

Stuart returned his attention to her. "If they'd asked for anyone else, anyone but Falcon, I would've left him behind. But they asked for you."

"Because I'm . . . a woman."

He got in her face. "Now that you've mentioned it, what the hell are you doing out here? This is no place for a woman."

Casey's mouth dropped open. She was taken aback, but only for a second; then she was all over him, flailing away, hitting Stuart again and again. He fell back, but she went after him, hammering away with her fists.

*The lousy bastard was leaving her behind. Her fa-
ther had gotten away with that, but Stuart would pay.
He would pay and pay and pay . . . .*

She tried to knee Stuart in the groin, but he caught
her hands and twisted her arms over her head. Casey
ended up dancing around on one foot. Laughter broke
out among the bandits, or maybe it was just the first
time she'd heard it.

Casey kicked back and connected with Stuart's shin.
He yelped and shoved her away. The bandit leader
caught her and pushed her into the arms of his men.
Casey stumbled but couldn't fall . . . because the bandits were fondling her breasts, groping her bottom,
reaching between her legs. They were touching everything except her hair. She screamed, and that caused
their leader to shout an order. His men backed away
as their leader took Casey by the hand and led her up
the ridge.

CHAPTER
SEVENTEEN

Colonel Gzap called Lieutenant Bien as he was pushing his men down the southeastern trail. They were several hundred meters beyond the split, jogging along, spread all the hell out.

"Where are you?"

Bien told him without looking at the map.

"And still no sign of the Americans?"

When Bien answered in the negative, the net went silent and stayed that way long enough to make Bien nervous. He pulled out his light and double-checked his position as he jogged along. Bien nodded to himself as he put the map and light away. His men were making fantastic time. They would come upon the Americans at any moment. And those who had dropped out along the way? He would deal with them later.

The mission came first. Something no one but he and Gzap seemed to understand. This American general was no ordinary prisoner, but someone who could be traded for the Americans' complete withdrawal from South Vietnam. Then they would settle with their puppets in Saigon.

Think of it! The two countries united as one. As it should've been years ago, immediately after his ancestors had chased the French out of the country. The Americans were the very last foreigners who would ever prop up a phony government in any part of his country. A phony government that had no more interest in the Vietnamese people than . . . .

Over the handset came, "Bien, tell your men to take a break."

Bien could not believe what he had heard, missed a step, and stumbled on the trail. "Stop? You want me to stop?"

"That is what I said."

The lieutenant had no idea what to make of the order. It was the first time Gzap had ever called a halt during any operation. Gzap's motto was hit them hard, hit them fast, and get out even faster. The Americans' firepower was awesome.

Bien did not have to tell his men twice. They stumbled to a halt, dropping along the trail. No one moved out as security so Bien passed some names down the column. One of those had fallen out along the way so he sent down another name. The second man muttered a curse, got to his feet, and moved away to become a sentry. Canteens were opened. When Bien heard that, he passed along word he would shoot the first man who cramped up and could not go on. The canteens were put away. His men had seen him do that before.

The colonel's voice crackled across the handset. "Bien, you should have caught them by now. The Americans are nowhere near Magic Mountain and they have not recrossed into Vietnam."

Bien had no answer for that. That was the one question he was least expecting.

Bien stood up and walked down the trail. "Er—I guess they were farther ahead of us than we thought. But we should catch them soon. What is that noise in the background?"

"The Americans are shelling us. They want you to know it is impossible for you to return to base camp. They probably have troops coming down the southeastern trail in your direction."

Bien looked behind him. The moon created shadows in the trees towering over him. If the Americans sent a reconnaissance-in-force down the southeastern trail . . . . He was down to what? Five or six men?

"So stay alert," said Gzap over the handset. "The platoon I sent to block the helicopter survivors from returning to Vietnam ran into heavy resistance on the east-west trail, and your reinforcements are involved in a firefight with the Americans at the base of Magic Mountain."

Bien did not hear him. He was staring at the trail. But for his footprints and the sentry's there were no others there. He pulled out his light and double-checked the trail, moving ahead of the sentry. The sentry hastily put away his canteen. Bien never saw the man. He was looking for prints. Boot prints. He saw none. Nothing on the trail ahead of him!

Bien ran down the trail. That was impossible! It had rained. There were puddles on the trail. But where were the prints?

"Bien! I am talking to you!" screamed Gzap.

"There are no footprints!" he blurted out.

"What do you mean? There have to be. You reported that it rained."

No answer from Bien. He was looking north, in the direction they had just come. In seconds, he had what was left of his men sweeping up both sides of the southeast trail, returning north. If the Americans had heard them coming and stepped off the trail . . . that had to be the answer. There were no footprints anywhere.

While his men conducted this search, Bien pulled out his map and found the trail leading to a Cambodian village, the trail where his men had found only the prints of bare feet. He had seen the prints himself . . . leading toward the river.

The Americans needed boats. They had wounded. Bien had seen the blood, but not lately. And no footprints. The bandage he had picked up was part of the charade!

The Americans had used a false trail to lose him. It was the oldest trick in the book, and it worked especially well on those traveling fast!

He slapped his map against his thigh and the sound echoed up the trail. The Americans had used his quickness against him, not to mention their reputation for never leaving their wounded behind. But the game was not over. Not yet. Think, fool! Where are they now?

As Gzap squawked over the handset, Bien studied the map again. The Americans were in boats taken from the Cambodian village. There was no reason to go there but to commandeer boats. And now the Americans were on their way downstream, returning to South Vietnam. There was only one way to stop them. It might not make his reputation, but it just might save his head.

Gzap was yelling at him. "Are you listening to me, soldier? I am talking to you."

Bien caught up with his men as they swept the flanks of the southeastern trail, and as he did, he explained to Gzap how the Americans had tricked him. It turned his stomach to do so, but he wanted to keep his head.

"I am leaving men to search the flanks of the southeastern trail while I take the others into the village. Alert the patrol boat below the shoals. It will be the only chance we have of stopping the Americans."

And, he did not have to add, saving his career.

✳   ✳   ✳

The bandits hustled the Americans into their boats and across the river. Lancaster was laid in the bottom of a boat. A bandit stepped on the unconscious man as he made his way to the bow, but none of the Americans protested his treatment. They were too busy climbing in themselves. A second guard slipped in each stern and the boats pushed off.

From the ridge Casey watched her former teammates complete their trip across the river, then almost trample the bandit in the bow to get ashore and disappear into the jungle. They brought Lancaster along and weren't careful how they did it.

She was a dead women. As dead as any woman could be and still be up and walking around. And she wouldn't be on her feet much longer. This so-called liberated woman was about to be reduced to a babbling idiot by a long line of men who'd never made it with a white woman. What asshole had said being a blonde was an asset in this business?

But she could decide how and when she died. That was something her father had tried to teach her: the importance of dying well. It was a lesson she'd laughed at as being overly melodramatic. She needed that lesson now.

Casey ignored the wolfish grins of her captors and looked around for some kind of weapon. Several of the bandits had followed their leader to the top of the ridge. No sloppy twenty-seconds for these bastards. Casey shrugged off the thought. It was counterproductive.

The radio lay at her feet. No weapon there. They'd never give her time to pick it up, much less time to club anyone over the head. Then Casey saw the pistol on the bandit leader's hip. The man had his back to her.

Now that was something she might be able to get her hands on. Was the bandit thinking more about getting laid than being had? The Cambodian was the same size as the man she'd flattened along the riverbank. There was only the strap across the butt, holding the pistol inside its holster. But she had to be quick—

A shout from below caused Casey to look in that direction. James Stuart still stood on her side of the river. She glanced at the far side. The rest of the team had already disappeared into the elephant grass. Stuart was saying something to the Cambodians surrounding him. He pointed to the ridge and started toward her.

Stuart wasn't leaving her behind! He'd gotten his men to safety. Now it was her turn.

A bandit ran down the ridge and thrust a rifle in Stuart's face. The American brushed the barrel aside and continued to the top of the ridge. Once there, he walked over to where Casey stood. When he did, the bandit leader stepped between Stuart and her.

It was hard for Casey to contain herself. She wanted to shove the little bastard aside, leap into Stuart's arms, and let him spirit her away. Instead, she waited to see what the lieutenant had in mind. The two of them were surrounded by bandits.

Stuart pointed at the radio and said something in Cambodian. The bandit leader shook his head. Stuart said something else, gestured at Casey, then gestured at the busted radio. The Cambodian shook his head again and pointed at the boats which had returned from ferrying the other members of the Blue Jay team across the river.

Casey's hopes fell with an almost audible sound. Stuart had returned for the damn radio. The son of a bitch had only come back for the radio. Damn him, and damn all military men and their obsession with lost equipment.

Blue Jay bent down and picked up the radio. When he stood up it was in the face of plenty of rifles, pistols, and knives. He turned the radio so the bandit leader

could see the holes across its back, then twisted the
knobs across the top. The radio made no sound.

The bandit leader shook his head again. Blue Jay
leaned down in the shorter man's face and shouted,
gesturing at the radio.

This was nuts, thought Casey. Stuart's going to get
us both killed.

The bandit leader unbuttoned the strap across his
holster so he could get at his pistol.

But so could Casey.

Now she realized what Stuart had in mind. He was
creating a diversion. If she took advantage of the diversion and went for the pistol, good, but if she didn't,
Stuart could back off, apologize, and then cross the
river and rejoin his men. This man wasn't going to shoot
Stuart. The bandit wanted those American supplies and
whatever he could swap for them on the black market
in Phnom Penh.

Casey chewed on her lip and stared at the pistol.
The bandits had no way of knowing she didn't know
how to fire the damn thing, that she'd resisted her
father's every attempt to teach her, had taken a per-
verse sort of pride in her ignorance. Another mistake
come back to haunt her. But all she had to do was
point the gun at their leader and everyone would fall in
line. The strap was off, the Cambodian's hand hovering over the butt. It was now or never.

Casey looked over the bandit leader's shoulder for
some signal from Blue Jay. Instead, she saw the lieutenant throw down the radio along with its handset
and whip antenna. Was that the signal?

When everyone, including Casey, looked up, they saw a grenade in Stuart's hand. The lieutenant removed the pin and held the grenade high over his head.

Mouths fell open, eyes bulged out. The American had a grenade! And it was armed! Where had it come from? And if he was crazy enough to return for a busted radio, what would he do with a grenade? Could they run for it? Was there time to leap to the riverbank below? But who could outrun a hand grenade?

Blue Jay dropped his hand, and every eye followed that hand. The grenade disappeared from Casey's sight, behind the bandit leader, then reappeared in an easy upward toss, soaring over everyone's head. Casey was as transfixed as anyone. The grenade seem to hang in the air.

But not long. When the grenade started its downward plunge, the bandits broke and ran, throwing down their weapons as they did. Most ran for the ridge, screaming and cursing those who got in their way. The bandit leader was the first over the side, rolling down to the riverbank below. Someone slammed into Casey and she fell backwards.

No! Stay on your feet! You have to get away from that grenade.

Instead, her feet flew out from under her. Casey thought she'd sit down hard, but she didn't sit at all. It appeared she had fallen into a hole. A bottomless pit.

Casey screamed as she fell off the ridge. She reached out for a handhold, anything to grab onto. There was nothing. Nothing at all! She twisted around to see where she was headed, but on this side of the ridge there were no torches, no illumination.

Overhead, the grenade exploded. Below the ridge Casey hit the river, stinging her from thigh to face. Casey gasped, took in a mouthful of water, and gagged. She tried to spit it out but couldn't. More water forced its way in. She was underwater and couldn't stop falling. Until she hit bottom. There she twisted her feet under her, planted them on the riverbed, and shot toward the surface.

Casey broke the surface gagging, spit out what she could, and retched even more. She coughed and looked around. The river was in darkness, pulling her downstream. There was a popping sound in the distance. Were her ears popping?

"They're shooting at us!" Stuart's face was a white spot in the darkness. "Get back under water!"

Casey did.

Standing on the riverbank the bandit leader finished emptying a rifle at the spot where he had last seen the Americans, then organized the remaining members of his band into two separate units. One group was ordered to take one of the boats across the river to recapture the Americans who had disappeared into the jungle; the second ordered to pull another boat around the net and relaunch it downstream.

The bandit leader ground his teeth. The American had made a fool of him, and in front of his men, and the son of a dog had returned for the woman. A blond-headed woman. Any whorehouse in Phnom Penh would pay good money for a woman with blond hair.

"What about our wounded?" A young bandit held a torch in one hand, a rifle in the other.

"If they were too stupid to throw themselves over the side of the ridge, they deserved to die." The bandit leader pointed at the boat now below the net. "Get in! We shall search the whole river if necessary. I want that woman."

The man with the torch glanced at the ridge overhead where the wounded cried for medical assistance. How many of his friends were up there? His cousin for sure. He had seen his cousin knocked down in the mad scramble to escape from the grenade. Was his cousin dead or only injured? And what would his family think if he left his cousin behind?

He touched his leader's shoulder. "I think—"

The bandit leader whirled around, and in the same motion slapped the young man across the face. "Get in the boat!" He jerked out his pistol. "Or you will join those on the ridge."

After the young man started for the boat below the net, the bandit leader turned to the men in the boat above the net. The slap had drawn their attention.

"What are you waiting for? Cross the river and return with the Americans. It should be easy. They are unarmed, and the Americans never leave their wounded behind. Use that weakness to your advantage."

The men nodded, then dug in with their paddles, and the boat shot across the river.

The bandit leader walked over and stepped into the boat below the net. As he did, he called for torches, then taunted his men when they didn't move quickly. "Do you honestly think we cannot recapture a white woman in this jungle?"

CHAPTER
EIGHTEEN

Across the river and fifty yards into the jungle, Pike and Eskew lowered the wounded Lancaster to the ground, then stood up.

"Okay, Pike, let's you and me go back and get some of those weapons."

"I'll come with you," offered Falcon.

"No, sir. Blue Jay said you're to stay here and take care of Lancaster."

Falcon glanced at the unconscious man, who was not about to go anywhere anytime soon. "But there's only two of you."

In the darkness, Pike flashed a smile no one could possibly see. "Then those bandits don't stand a chance. They'll never get more than five or six guys in one of those little boats of theirs."

Both men pulled out their boot knives and disappeared toward the river, leaving Falcon with the unconscious Lancaster. Rank had its privileges, but if

Falcon overrode the field commander, Blue Jay in this case, it might cost him his life, and the death of the CIC would be counterproductive to the war effort.

Falcon looked around. There was a moon out but to little effect. More than ten years ago, he'd spent his first night in the jungle. Some animal had run down a tree, leaped on his hammock, landing on his leg, then jumped to the ground and run off in the jungle. He'd awakened with a start, jumped out of bed, forgetting where he was, and fallen on his face. He could still feel where the animal had landed, and he always wondered what kind of animal it had been. Detailed to South Vietnam, he'd wondered a good deal about what kind of animal it had been. Absentmindedly, he rubbed the spot on his leg as he scanned the night. To tell the truth, he'd never seen it so dark before. By now he was usually in Long Bien reviewing the day's progress reports. And body count.

Falcon snorted. Body count. The secretary of defense was obsessed with the body count, always asking about the "numbers." It was as if the man thought he could run this war like an automobile production line, which was the last job the secretary of defense had held. Torches left the far side of the river and headed in his direction. Lord, he never thought he'd come this close to being one of those numbers.

The bandits found where the Americans had fought their way through the overgrowth along the river and into an open space, then through waist-high grass. The path was well marked. Pike and Eskew had made sure of that.

The bandits moved slowly and loudly. While crossing the river they had decided to let the Americans know they were about to be recaptured. The light from the torch would do that; the noise, too. The Americans would have no choice but to drop their wounded and run for the border. Recapturing the wounded American would be better than facing their leader empty-handed. No one wanted that, but neither did they want to take on those crazy Americans—especially after seeing what their lieutenant had done with that grenade. Cries of their wounded floated across the river to them.

As the last bandit passed Pike, the American rose out of the elephant grass, put an arm across the man's neck, tilted his head back, and slit the bandit's throat. He lowered his victim to the ground and snatched the rifle out of his hand. He laid the weapon beside the corpse, then moved on to the next man, wiping the bloody knife on his fatigue pants.

The next bandit carried a torch high over his head, as if the light would shield him from danger. He hung back from the others and glanced from side to side as he moved through the tall grass. Minutes earlier, he had hesitated, and the man stepping off the boat behind him had cursed and moved ahead with a rough shove. So when the torchbearer glanced over his shoulder at a man approaching from the rear, he expected more of the same. Instead, a knife was planted in his back.

Pike rammed the blade in hard, all the way through the skinny man's body. The bandit tried to scream but found he couldn't even breathe. He reached up, found the tip of the blade protruding from the left side of his chest and passed out—before dying. Pike snatched the torch from the unconscious man's hand and lowered him to the ground.

There was a shout up ahead, followed by a scream, and Willie Tee hollered, "Coming your way!"

The bandit who had slipped away from Eskew was halfway between the two Americans. Having heard the shout behind him, the bandit glanced back to see if anyone was gaining on him. He ran full-force into Pike's knife. Pike was shoved back a step or two, but he dug in and pushed back. He stood the bandit straight up, then threw him off his knife and onto the ground.

"What's the matter, Willie Tee? Can't hold up your end of the bargain?"

Wiping the blade on his pants leg, Pike stared at the bandit lying at his feet. In the light from the dying torch, he saw the man he'd killed was only a boy. A kid lay on his back in a pool of blood, staring into a night he couldn't see, at stars he'd never see again, a moon he'd never see again . . . .

Pike spit along the trail. How old was this damn kid anyway? "Old enough to blow you away" would be the standard reply around any American campfire. But that didn't give Pike any satisfaction. He'd still killed a damn kid.

What was a twelve- or thirteen-year-old kid doing out here? Probably been conned into joining up. Probably been told all he had to do was laze along the river and wait for his fellow countrymen to come along and fall into their net, and make them pay the toll. Nothing to it. Cambodians were used to being kicked around by Charlie, so why not do some of that kicking themselves, and make some dough in the process?

And the boy had believed them. Just as Pike had believed he was defending America against the godless communist hordes. Until he arrived in 'Nam and found himself killing men, women, and children more dedicated to a cause than Pike could ever be dedicated—to turning them back. And the more he killed, the more Uncle Ho sent down that damned trail named for him.

Was Blue Jay right? Could they kill enough Charlies to make Charlie think twice about making the trip south? Pike shook his head. Not unless Uncle Ho made the trip himself, and because Uncle Ho never had to face their guns or knives, he could go merrily along sending more men, women, and children down that damn trail to their deaths.

At first, Pike had taken to Blue Jay's strategy, sticking it to Charlie before Charlie could stick it to them. He'd liked that. But now another kid was dead, and all Pike could think about was how sick and tired he was of all this killing. The trick was finding a way to survive the remainder of his tour without being killed by some officer working his way up the career ladder on the backs of dead GIs. Blue Jay said he had a contact who could get him base camp duty. All he had to do was ask. Okay, he'd ask—once they were out of this mess, and what a mess it was. This playing hero could get you killed.

Pike stripped a couple of the men—but not the boy—of their weapons, their gear, and their clothing. The boy's face he covered with a dead man's jacket, then rejoined Falcon and Eskew on their knees beside Lancaster. The two men were trimming shafts of bamboo and making a litter. They worked quickly and silently in the light from one of the bandits' flashlights.

Eskew looked up. "We're going to need some clothes to tie it together."

"Way ahead of you." Pike tossed the bandits' clothing toward him.

Eskew snatched the pajamas out of the air and sorted through the garments, most of them shirts. He came away with blood all over his hands. He looked at Pike, who was now on his knees disassembling one of the captured rifles: an old Enfield, a very sturdy and reliable weapon.

"You couldn't've brought me some pants?" asked Eskew. "I'm sure they wouldn't have minded, and the pants might not've been covered with all this blood."

Pike drew back in mock horror. "Pull down a man's pants? No, sirree, Willie Tee, my ma didn't raise any perverts."

"Do we know where we're headed?" asked Falcon.

"Yes, sir," Eskew said without taking his attention from the shirts he was slicing apart. "Blue Jay's going to board one of Charlie's boats downstream and use its radio to advise Long Bien of our rendezvous point."

Falcon only nodded, but Pike said, "Then I wish him luck. If that damn blonde didn't get him killed going back for her, she'll damn well do it making a try for that patrol boat. I've never seen anyone who draws fire like that blonde does."

*　　*　　*

Casey and Stuart came out of the river six hundred yards below the bandits' ambush site. Stuart dragged Casey ashore where they collapsed in the bushes. Once he let her go, Casey was on him, hammering him with her fists.

"You bastard! You made me think . . . you were going . . . to leave me . . . back there."

Stuart rolled away. "Hey! I didn't know . . . if you could pull it off."

Casey came after him on all fours, flattening bushes as she followed Stuart along the riverbank, hammering his backside as he tried to crawl away. "Next time . . . tell me . . . what's going on."

He rolled over, hands coming up to protect himself. "Okay! Uncle!"

"I'm part of this and don't you fucking forget it."

Blue Jay stared at her where he lay. "Yes, I do believe you are."

*　　*　　*

Lieutenant Bien's platoon arrived at the ambush site in the remaining boats from the upstream village. Bien took little time negotiating for the boats. When the village chief protested, Bien shot him dead on the spot. The NVA floated away to the wails of the dead man's family.

The ambush site was ablaze with torches, and on

the ridge, Bien found bandits who had been left behind, most of them dead.

"What happened here?" he asked.

"Help me!" A wounded bandit clutched his stomach from which he was bleeding. "I am hurt. Hurt bad."

Bien knelt down and lifted the man's head. "And you will certainly die unless you receive proper medical attention. My medic will treat you, but only after you have told me what has happened here. Leave nothing out."

"Please! My stomach . . . the pain."

Bien stood up, dropping the man's head to the ground.

The bandit screamed, and it was not very long before Bien knew everything that had occurred before he and his men arrived at the ambush site.

Across the river they found dead men in the grass. They also found where the Americans had constructed a litter for their wounded. Bien gathered his men around him and took out his light and his map. On the far side of the river, the wounded bandit screamed for the medic, but the medic was with his lieutenant. There was still a chance to recapture the general. They must not lose their last chance to become heroes.

Bien moved a finger across the map. "There are plenty of places to hide, but only one trail where they can make any serious progress returning to Vietnam. The Americans seem to be familiar with this side of the border so they will naturally use this trail. They may have used it before. From the tracks you can see there are only three of them, and one of them has a bad leg. The other two carry the stretcher."

"Under those circumstances I would take the trail, too," said one of his men, stating the obvious.

Bien stared at the soldier, who was usually much brighter. Maybe the forced march had addled his brain. Or everyone was feeling the pressure of losing the American general.

Not only did they need time to move ahead of the Americans, but time to locate them, and time to set an ambush, a very delicate matter indeed.

"Sir," said one of his men, breaking into Bien's thoughts. "An old trader's trail runs here." The soldier pushed his finger along a line paralleling the route along which Eskew and Pike were carrying Lancaster's litter. "It was well traveled until the capitalists came." The soldier glanced across the river. "By honest traders. Not this Cambodian scum. I traveled it myself with my uncle."

Bien's eyes brightened. "Can you find it?"

"Possibly. It is probably overgrown now."

The lieutenant stood up, his men following his lead. "It is our only chance. You must find that trail."

"I would need a light—"

"And you shall have it!"

Minutes later, they were headed northeast and Bien was on the radio with Colonel Gzap. He brought his commanding officer up to date and told him what he proposed to do.

"Good," Gzap said, "and when you find the Americans, kill them. Kill them all."

"The general, too?"

"We cannot risk losing him again."

"But I think I can take him alive. I have a plan."

"Bien, are you going to do as I ordered?"

The lieutenant sighed. "Yes, sir. When I find the Americans I will kill all of them, including the general."

CHAPTER
NINETEEN

Robert Sligh and his Viet Cong guide stopped at a taxi stand in the middle of Long Bien, a village expanding rapidly with the enlargement of the American compound. The VC climbed down from the pedicab. He did not offer to pay its driver, and before Sligh could remember to do so, the pedicab was gone.

"This way," his guide said.

As the two men walked down a street, Sligh noticed they were not being mobbed by children and beggars. They turned into an alleyway, approaching a taxi cab from the rear, its engine running and its driver apparently asleep. When they climbed inside, the cab lurched forward before Sligh could close the door. The car was a twenty-year-old Renault with a front seat that didn't match its rear one. A side window was missing its glass, and the rearview mirror was tilted so the driver couldn't see his passengers.

Sligh's guide said, "You will have to conform to our security regulations."

"How's that?" said the reporter with a laugh. "You blindfold me and we drive around until I lose my sense of direction?"

"That will not be necessary. Just sit on the floorboard." The Viet Cong smiled. "Then we will drive around until you lose your sense of direction."

"Fine with me."

Sligh slid down on the floorboard, and the Vietnamese pulled his feet up, giving the American more leg room. The VC took a piece of black cloth out of his satchel and handed it to the reporter.

"I thought you said I wasn't going to wear a blindfold."

"Not for now, but for when you leave the cab."

Sligh stuffed the blindfold in his pocket. Didn't they have any other color in this damn country? When he returned to the States he was going to throw out everything he owned that was black, even his damn wing tips.

The cabbie took a hard left, then a right, veered off to the left again, and switched right and then left twice before proceeding in a straight line.

"That's enough," Sligh said in Vietnamese. "I'm lost."

Both the driver and the guide laughed, but Sligh was considering what he was about to do as he leaned against the car door. He was about to enter the American compound illegally. The army wouldn't be pleased and he would likely end up in the stockade. He might lose his credentials, get kicked out of Vietnam, and limit his possibilities of being employed, except by the supermarket tabloids.

He had to have a backup. He didn't like it, but he had to make sure this story was reported by someone. After considering the competition, Sligh decided there was only one person he could possibly manipulate, so he pulled out his notebook, pen, and penlight. He turned the penlight on, stuck the light in his mouth, and started writing. Composing a point, he looked up to see the Viet Cong watching him.

The reporter took the light from his teeth. "I'm writing what you've told me. I want you to give it to another reporter if I fail to return to the tailor's hut by noon tomorrow."

"A very good idea, but make no mention of the tunnel."

"And don't fool around getting this story to her."

"A woman?"

"Yeah, but she can handle it."

"Who is she, Mr. Sligh?"

"Casey Blackburn. She reports for one of the wire services. By Monday morning the whole country will know about the invasion."

The VC leaned forward. "Is this the same Casey Blackburn who interviewed Ho Chi Minh?"

"Yes," Sligh said, a flatness coming into his voice.

"Then I will make sure Miss Blackburn has this story. No one told me Casey Blackburn was in Saigon."

"She's only been here a week or so. It's her first combat assignment. She hardly knows her way around. I've had to answer a lot of her questions."

"Yes, yes, but Casey Blackburn. She will make sure this story is told. Miss Blackburn is against this war as much as you are."

Oh shit! thought Sligh. Some bitch sweet-talks her way into an interview with Uncle Ho and she becomes an instant expert. Next thing you know she'll be doing TV.

The Viet Cong was watching him. "Mr. Sligh, your note for Miss Blackburn . . . ."

"Oh, yeah. I was just about finished."

"I will be sure Miss Blackburn has it."

"Yes. I'm sure you will."

Sligh finished his story, all the time thinking when he was released from the stockade, that young woman was going to owe him more than a good steak dinner. Dammit! Why did this shit always happen to him?

Sligh kept the story as sparse and unemotional as possible, going back and striking out several phrases his editors had blue-lined in previous stories. Then he wrote an accompanying note.

Casey,

I'm being held prisoner inside the American compound at Long Bien. If you hate this war as much as you say you do, see that the attached story reaches the States for the Sunday editions.

When I get out of the stockade, I want to see my name on the byline and in front of yours.

Robert Sligh

PS Fuck TV!

Sligh looked up to see the Vietnamese staring out the window. He tapped the man on the knee and handed him the story along with the note. The VC put both the note and the story in his satchel, then spoke sharply to their driver. The cab turned around and headed in the opposite direction.

Well, thought Sligh, that meant they weren't anywhere near the tunnel. This was an excellent opportunity to gather more material for his book, a book that would possibly win the Pulitzer Prize and put him out of reach of mere editors. He asked, "Have you any relatives fighting in this war or is there just you?"

The Viet Cong stared at Sligh for the longest. Hell, maybe the gook didn't understand the question, or the importance of the Pulitzer Prize.

"I have an older sister who is a nurse in the base camp the Americans are shelling."

Sligh didn't say anything. If this was going to be the same old bullshit . . . .

"That, and the fact that I speak English are probably the reasons I was chosen to bring this information to you."

"Where'd you learn your English?"

"I have a job working for the Americans."

Sligh knew better than to continue with that line of questioning. It would take him nowhere, and possibly make the gook think *he* was stupid. "Why'd you and your sister become involved with the Party?"

"For the same reason my two dead brothers did. Our father was too outspoken. When the Diems had heard enough, he was thrown into jail."

"Tortured?"

"He may as well have been. My father was diabetic,

and the guards refused to allow my mother to see him. In a few days, he fell into a coma and died. The Diems knew my father was a diabetic. His blood is on their hands."

"Diem and his brother are dead."

"So is John Kennedy, but his lackeys continue this war. So do my sister and I."

The taxi jerked to a stop.

"Please put on the blindfold, Mr. Sligh, and remember you are going into a highly restricted area. I will have to check the blindfold before you sit up."

Sligh did as he was told. Once the blindfold was in place he felt the VC's fingers around the edges, tugging it up or down, cutting out all light. The reporter was helped to his feet and out of the car. Along the way, he bumped his head on the door frame. A voice from somewhere in front of them whispered "hurry." A woman's voice. The taxi was already pulling away.

After a few tentative steps, his guide said, "Please lower your head."

He did. Once inside, the noises of the street became muffled. That in itself was strange, as the Vietnamese used little material to shut out noise. Off to his left the woman spoke again, asking them to follow her. Sligh was led across the room, then taken on a quick left, followed by a longer right. He noted the pungent smell of rice being cooked as only the Vietnamese can cook it, the vibrations of trucks rumbling along the side of the house, and the giggles of children in a room Sligh passed.

His guide held him up. "Stop here. Please do not

move. You are in front of the entrance of the tunnel and it is a rather long drop."

Sligh stopped moving. He even stopped breathing.

There was a scraping noise as pieces of wood were dragged away; then wood was dropped on the far side of the room. By the sound it made landing, Sligh could tell the floor was made of dirt.

"I will take the blindfold off when you are inside the tunnel." There was a bumping sound at the reporter's feet. "Now I want you to sit down on the edge of the hole and slide your legs over the side. Once you are sitting down, I will position the ladder under your feet."

"Gotcha."

With the help of his guide and a second pair of hands, Sligh sat down, stuck his feet inside the hole, and bumped into something on his right.

"I will go down first. You will follow."

His guide let go of him, but the woman's hands stayed tightly on his arm. How deep was this damn hole anyway?

The guide's feet scuffled on the ladder as he made his way down. Moments later, the top rung was maneuvered under the reporter's feet.

"This is going to be tough to do with this blindfold on." Sligh raised his hands. "What if I took it off?"

A third person, someone who'd not made a sound since Sligh had entered the room, did now, working the action of a weapon. The reporter quickly lowered his hands.

"Please, Mr. Sligh," his guide said from below. "Do as we ask."

"I certainly will."

Sligh turned around and positioned his feet on the second or third rung of the ladder while the woman's hands steadied him from above. Then he took slow steps down, fumbling with his hands for the top of the ladder, and finding it. As Sligh moved down, the woman's hands let go, but by then his guide had him from below, his hands under the reporter's rump.

There were ten rungs before the VC said, "Last step."

Sligh stepped down, felt around with his feet, and finding solid ground, turned loose of the ladder.

"Down on your knees," said his guide, "and I will take off the blindfold. From here we will move on all fours. You may find the tunnel a tight fit as it was built for our people, not yours."

Sligh eased himself down, feeling the coolness of the ground with his hands and through his pants at the knees. He reached up and ripped the blindfold off. No way he was comfortable being on his hands and knees with a fucking blindfold on. The opening overhead went black as boards were placed over it. Sligh blinked, rubbed his eyes, and looked around.

He was in a pit about ten feet across. Lighting came from bulbs hanging from a cord along the walls, and the walls were shored up with planks. Printed on the planks was: A Gift from the People of the United States. Directly ahead of Sligh was the tunnel. It had a four-foot mouth, walls shored up by timbers, and a dirt floor. More lights disappeared into the darkness. Way off in the distance. If the army could see this. And the son of a bitch led right into their command center.

"How long it is?" asked Sligh, trying to keep the

excitement out of his voice.

"Over three hundred meters."

"Three hundred . . . meters?" Three hundred meters was longer than three football fields. Hell, the war might be over before he reached the other end.

His guide went on to explain. "We were lucky the builder of the tunnel understood your people and their expansionist ways. Since its completion, your countrymen have moved their perimeter out another one hundred and fifty meters." The VC pointed at the entrance. "This opening is now less than one hundred meters from the new perimeter."

"And you're building another tunnel to connect with this one when they expand the perimeter once again."

The Viet Cong only smiled.

"Where does it come out?"

"In the middle of the garbage dump. Your people do not like handling garbage. My people do all of that."

"I thought the garbage was hauled out daily."

"It is impossible to haul the garbage away as fast as your countrymen produce it." The Viet Cong paused. "There must be some very large garbage dumps in your country, Mr. Sligh."

"I'll send you Vance Packard's book." The Vietnamese didn't know who Vance Packard was, but instead of explaining, the reporter said, "I'm ready to go."

"Very well." And the Viet Cong scampered into the tunnel.

At first Sligh could keep up with the man, even in places where it was a tight fit, but after the first hundred meters—the first football field—Sligh's shoulders begin to ache and his hands and knees stung from being nicked and scraped. And he'd snagged a few splinters along the way. Still his guide moved on at the same easy pace, leaving Sligh farther and farther behind.

It seemed like an eternity when Sligh plodded into a turnaround, raised his head, and took in the small area. His guide was waiting for him, canteens in each hand, and a warm smile on his face.

Where the hell had the canteens come from? He didn't remember . . . .

"Halfway point, Mr. Sligh."

"Then it doesn't make sense . . . to go back . . . does it?"

The VC offered him one of the canteens.

As Sligh took a seat on an empty ammo box, his knees came up in his face and his head brushed the ceiling. Dirt dribbled down on him. After brushing the dirt out of his hair, he took the canteen and gulped down the water.

"Not too much. You cramp in here and I don't know how we would get you out."

Sligh pulled the canteen away and returned it to his guide. The Vietnamese put the top back on the canteen without taking a drink.

"You're not having any?"

"The water is for you, Mr. Sligh."

"Then have some so I won't cramp up."

The Vietnamese smiled. "Thank you." During sips, he noticed the American rubbing his knees and picking at a splinter in one of his fingers. "Worth the effort?"

"Going to be." Sligh wiped his face on his sleeve and saw the dirt smear left behind. If anyone had told him he'd be spending the weekend crawling through a tunnel that led into the American command center, he would've told them they were nuts. But in the next breath he would've asked when they could get started.

They sat in the rest area a few more minutes before moving on. After the next hundred yards, Sligh couldn't think, couldn't do anything but plod along and stare at the next light. He promised his hands, knees, and shoulders that they would earn a rest if they only carried him a little farther—say, down to the next light. And Sligh's hands, knees, and shoulders never forgave him for breaking each and every one of his promises. He thumped and bumped into the walls as he lumbered along. Occasionally he smashed bulbs and knocked down support beams, but still he plodded on.

Just think of the story. Just think of the damn story. Just think of the dummies dicking around in Saigon instead of following up a good lead. Next week, your back won't hurt, the cuts and bruises will've healed, and those same dumb-asses will be congratulating you on your scoop. Yeah. Buying you drinks, slapping you on the back, and hating your guts. That'll be the very best part of all.

One of Sligh's arms collapsed and he went down on a shoulder and the side of his face. Jammed against the wall, he lay there, rump in the air and the side of his face in the ground, and telling himself it was only the story that mattered, only the name on the byline that counted, not the numbness in his shoulders or the dull stumps that had once been his hands.

He forced himself to his hands and knees and looked down the tunnel where his guide waited for him. The man had been doing a good bit of that lately. Sligh took a breath and floundered on, hands and knees raw nubs of pain. Besides the aches and pains, Sligh was dirty, as were his clothes.

He stared at the VC waiting for him up ahead. *You're so damn proud of this tunnel you've forgotten about the dirt. The army will know I came through a tunnel. Then what'll you do? They're sure to come looking for you and your damn tunnel.*

At the next rest area, Sligh collapsed on another ammo box, closed his eyes, and tried to catch his breath. His arms were lead weights at his sides, and he didn't think he could hold up his head. Would the VC notice the dirt and try to stop him from going topside?

Just let the little bastard try! He'd kill the son of a bitch, if he could raise his hands to fasten them around the little man's throat.

"How much . . . farther?"

"We're here."

Sligh opened his eyes. "Thank God!"

There was another Vietnamese there. Sligh would've jerked back in surprise if he'd had the energy—and the room. The second VC sat beside the guide, a pack in his lap, a canteen on top of the pack, and under the canteen, a pistol. An old German Mauser.

"You can go up once you have cleaned yourself," said his guide.

"Cleaned . . . myself?"

"We have a towel and water, and some fatigues. They

should be your size." The man's tone changed. "Mr. Sligh, I only hope you can do as much to protect this tunnel as we are doing to help you. My people have some very special plans for this tunnel."

Sligh shook his head as he took the washcloth. "You people think of everything, don't you."

"We have to. We're playing for very high stakes: the reunification of our country."

Fifteen minutes later, Sligh was topside and the tunnel was being closed up behind him. That was of little matter. Sligh had already sighted in on a couple of reference points and paced off the distance to both of them before heading for the command bunker.

After Sligh disappeared in the darkness, more Vietnamese, those who hadn't allowed the Americans to force them to leave the compound, stepped out of the darkness and began dumping sacks of dirt down the hole. While they worked topside, the tunnel was shored up from below by VC who'd followed Sligh and his guide through from the other end. Minutes later, the spur had been blocked off from below, filled in from above, and completely covered with garbage.

CHAPTER TWENTY

I t took Casey and Stuart almost an hour to locate the North Vietnamese patrol boat. With very little moon and another outburst from the clouds they were practically on top of the craft before Blue Jay realized the square corners of the cabin couldn't be part of the jungle. He pulled Casey behind a tree, and when he pointed out the structure, she saw a blackened hull with a flat cabin top. It was moored parallel to the riverbank. The patrol boat was about forty feet long, wider than a Huey, and had a .50-caliber machine gun mounted on the bow. The machine gun covered the river. The night was quiet but for the cicadas and crickets and the river lapping against the boat's hull. It had even stopped raining.

Casey leaned into Stuart. "Why are they so near the bank? If they were in the middle we'd have to swim out to them."

"Against the bank they blend into the darkness."

Muffled laughter came from below deck, and moments later, the hatch opened and a sailor stepped out. Casey noticed no light followed the man when he came topside. The Vietnamese stretched and moved around on deck. When he lit a cigarette, another sailor popped up from the other side of the cabin and spoke to him sharply. Casey and Blue Jay looked at each other. Neither had seen the man on the far side of the boat.

The smoker took a long drag off the cigarette and flicked it over the side . . . over the head of the man who had chastised him. From that moment on, the two sailors stood on opposite sides of the boat, backs to each other, the former cigarette smoker staring at the tree Casey and Stuart were hiding behind. Casey couldn't believe the Charlie couldn't see them. He stood less than ten feet away.

Minutes later, these two were joined by two more sailors from below deck, and they, too, stretched after coming topside. The last two walked around to the far side of the boat, one of them firing questions at the hidden guard. After hearing the replies, the questioner waved off the answers and returned below deck. His companion followed him.

The guard stood up and walked around to the side of the boat nearest Casey and Stuart. He gave his rifle to the man who'd tried to light the cigarette, then went below but not before speaking curtly to the new guard. The new guard said nothing, but as soon as the hatch closed, he lit up again, his only concession to security being that he cupped his hand over his cigarette as he strolled around the deck.

"What were they talking about?" whispered Casey.

"Us."

"What?" She glanced at the boat. "But how'd they know . . . ?"

"The men we tricked into following the false trail must've realized that's just what it was, then figured which way we were headed and called ahead."

"Then the bandits ambushing us . . . ." Casey was staring at the .50-caliber machine gun mounted on the bow. "Their slowing us down saved our lives."

"It also means Charlie will soon be arriving at the ambush site, maybe already has, and learned which way Falcon's headed. I've got to get on that boat. Stay here, Casey."

"But I could help."

Gripping her arm, Stuart leaned into her. "There's nothing you can do so stay behind the tree."

Casey opened her mouth, then shut it. If Falcon was willing to follow Stuart's lead, she should, too. "Just be careful."

"And you stay behind this tree. I want to know where you are at all times."

"Yes, sir!" she said in a muffled whisper.

Stuart stared at her for a moment, then shook his head before weaving his way through the underbrush and over to the riverbank, where he eased himself into the water. As he waded to the boat, the guard continued to lean against the far side of the cabin and stare over the river, puffing away on his cigarette. Stuart was pulling himself up on the near side of the boat when a shout came from below deck. Casey jumped back and grabbed the tree. Blue Jay slid back into the river, under the bow, where he stood in water up to his waist.

The guard flicked his cigarette over the side, then came around to stand over Stuart. The guard was listening to the sailors arguing below deck.

What were they saying? Casey hit the tree with her fist. Damn but she wished she could speak the frigging language.

The hatch was thrown open and one of the sailors stormed up, carrying a rifle. He joined the other guard, but only after slamming the hatch behind him. The sound echoed up and down the river. The two guards stood together, one mumbling, the other listening. Finally, the new guard stalked off, the old guard following him and lighting up another cigarette.

Casey looked at Blue Jay hunched over in the water under the hull. With two armed men prowling the deck Stuart was going nowhere.

She could feel the minutes tick by as the two sailors wandered around, muttering to each other and paying little attention to the river they were supposed to be surveilling. While she was standing there, the rest of the team was waiting for a chopper that would never come. Willie Tee would be forced to give up on Stuart and recross the border with an unconscious man in tow and Charlie on their heels. And when those Charlies caught up with them, Lancaster would be the first to die. She had seen that with the helicopter pilots.

She stepped from behind the tree. "Help me! Please help me!"

Blue Jay motioned her back behind the tree. The two guards dropped behind the far side of the cabin and peered around its corners.

"Help me!" Casey called out, and she didn't have to fake her nervousness. She raised her hands over her head and moved toward the boat, weaving her way through the clutter of underbrush.

Blue Jay stood up in the water, jabbing his finger in the direction of the jungle behind her. "Get back there," came his hoarse whisper.

There was a quick exchange between the guards, and one of them called to the sailors below. A chair screeched across the deck and fell to the floor as the other two rushed topside. Light flashed from the hatch, blinding her. Then the light went out. The two guards crept from behind the cabin, all the while looking for whoever else might be out there. They didn't see Stuart shake his head, then slip around to the far side of the boat.

A flashlight beam hit Casey in the face, and again she couldn't see where she was going. She could hear the men on the boat, but had no idea what they were doing. She forced herself to walk toward the boat, hands still over her head and her stomach doing flip-flops. The bandits had been a piece of cake compared to this.

Casey didn't see a limb and hit her forehead. Stunned, she went to one knee, then threw up her hands again. "Don't shoot! I'm the press!"

There was a sharp command from one of the sailors, and a gangplank was fitted between boat and shore. The flashlight was used to motion her aboard, along with some useless commands in Vietnamese. Casey crossed the plank, and when she stepped on deck, she saw Blue Jay on the far side of the cabin. He was slitting the throat of the rear guard.

Casey shivered. Killing people in cold blood. But they had to have that chopper for Lancaster.

Stuart grabbed the guard's rifle and eased the dead man to the deck.

Would he use the rifle on the rest of the sailors? Not with her in the line of fire. She had to get out of the line of fire.

A sailor grabbed Casey by the arm, ran the light up and down her, and then stuck the light in her face. She couldn't see anything but felt hands fingering her hair, gripping her arms, and holding her in place. She couldn't move. She couldn't get out of the line of fire.

The sailors shifted the light from her eyes. Casey blinked, and through the yellow blur, saw Blue Jay take another sailor from behind. As this man went down, his rifle clunked to the deck. The other two whipped around and saw the American dropping their comrade. A glance at the far end of the boat and they saw the rear guard was missing.

One of the Vietnamese leaped for the rifle and Blue Jay jumped him. The sailor threw up an arm, taking Stuart's knife across the forearm. Then the sailor got his hands on Stuart's wrist, and they hit the deck, rolling around, fighting over the knife.

The other sailor jerked out a pistol and pointed it and the flashlight at the two men rolling around on the deck. Before he could get off a shot, Casey gave him a shove and he went over the side. The flashlight dropped to the deck and the sailor went spread-eagled into the shallows.

Casey grabbed the shoulder of the man wrestling with Blue Jay and tried to pull him off. Stuart took this opportunity to twist the knife up and around and plant it in the Vietnamese's chest.

Casey stepped back, hand at her mouth. "No!"

"Yes!" said Blue Jay, working the knife in.

He threw the man off, and the sailor rolled over on his back. The Vietnamese looked at her, puzzled, said something, and died.

"But I didn't mean . . . ."

"I did!"

Blue Jay scrambled to his feet and reached for the guard's rifle. As he did, the sailor Casey had shoved into the shallows stuck his pistol over the side and took a shot at him. The bullet ran across Stuart's chest and dug into his shoulder, twisting the American to one side. Stuart stumbled forward and reached for the rifle, but his injured arm gave way, and his momentum carried him over the side.

The sailor slogged around in the waist-high water and fired at the spot where Stuart disappeared. When the American didn't surface, the Vietnamese turned the pistol on Casey and said something.

Something like "stay where you are," thought Casey, her worse fear realized. She was out here in this jungle all alone. Why hadn't she stayed behind the damn tree?

The sailor tried to climb over the side, but couldn't do it and still keep the pistol trained on Casey. He finally gave up and walked backwards through the shallows, making his way toward shore, never once taking his eyes off her, until he looked down to find the gangplank.

Casey figured this was about as good as it was going to get. She turned and ran for the other side of the boat. The pistol went off and wood splintered off the cabin as she dashed around the corner. Making the turn, her feet slipped from under her and she went down on the deck as the sailor thumped across the gangplank.

Casey scrambled to her feet and kept moving. When she looked back to see where the Vietnamese was, she tripped over the edge and went head over heels into the river. She hit with a splash, sank to the bottom, and stayed there, holding onto the hull to stay underwater.

Now what? She'd been too frightened to take much of a breath, and there was no way she could swim to the other side of the river. She had to have some air. But from where? Only one place: the far side of the boat. Charlie would never look for her there. After taking a deep breath, she could swim for the other side of the river or pick up the current in the middle. Certainly she could make the middle, but she had to have some air.

Casey felt her way under the boat, only coming to the surface when she thought her lungs would burst. She exploded to the surface to find herself nose-to-nose with someone. She yelped before recognizing James Stuart, his face tight with pain.

He said, "Swim to the middle and catch the current. I'll meet you downstream . . . this side of the river."

"You coming?"

"Just . . . a little bit slower."

The Vietnamese peered over the side and found Casey and her blond hair with his light. Stuart splashed water in the sailor's face. Casey ducked again, but even under water, she heard the pistol bark once, then twice.

Casey used weeds to pull herself under the boat. When she surfaced on the other side, she snatched a quick breath and started for the far side of the river. Stuart might be dead for all she knew, but his advice still held. Get downstream and get ashore. They'd never find her in the jungle.

Casey reached out with both hands and pulled back, then kicked hard and swam through the darkness, lungs burning. She wasn't in shape for this anymore than she'd been in shape to be force-marched across Cambodia. When she thought her lungs would burst, she shot to the surface and snatched another breath. Behind her, the pistol exploded and Casey dove under again. Moments later, the current caught her and she didn't have to resurface until well downstream.

Casey looked behind her. Was the boat coming? No. It was still moored along the riverbank with someone running around on deck.

Blue Jay? Couldn't be. Not after being shot. He wouldn't be able to climb aboard. And there was no way he'd be able to drag himself out of the river with the force of the rainy season runoff. Casey fought the river, trying to swim back upstream. She would hold her place in the middle of the river and wait for Stuart to show up.

"Stuart!"

No answer.

"Stuart! Where are you?"

No answer again.

"Blue Jay! Are you there?" Casey could hear the desperate tone in her voice.

"Coming your way," came his very weak reply.

"I can't see you. Can you mark your position?" *Mark your position?* Now where had that come from?

The wounded man slapped the water ten yards in front of her and closer to shore. Casey swam over and cut him off, then mistakenly hooked him by his wounded arm. Blue Jay let her know about it.

"Sorry!" She switched to the other side but wasn't satisfied with that either. "Turn over on your back, then we'll swim ashore."

"Now that's . . . positive thinking," gasped the wounded man as they were swept downstream.

"Just shut up and do it!"

Blue Jay shifted around on his back and Casey looped her arm under his chin, then Stuart kicked and Casey pulled, digging into the water with her free hand. It took forever, but forty to fifty yards downstream they were in the shallows, floundering ashore. They crawled up on the riverbank and fell into the weeds.

"No," gasped Blue Jay. "Got to get . . . farther inland. Boat's got . . . fifty caliber . . . . rip an arm . . . leg off."

Casey helped Stuart to his feet and they fumbled through a hedgerow, then tripped and fell in a pool of brackish backwater. Finally they crawled over an embankment and rolled down into some elephant grass.

"Damn!" moaned Blue Jay as he came to rest on his back. "Rescued by a damsel in distress."

"I—I owed you one."

"It's—it's not the same."

"You damn . . . pig!"

Blue Jay's laughter was cut short by the sound of the approaching patrol boat. Casey crawled to the top of the embankment. She had no idea what she'd do if the sailor decided to come ashore. The man had his pistol and probably a rifle or two. Stuart tried to follow her but didn't make it. He rolled back down the embankment, groaning in pain.

"Stay down there," ordered Casey.

"I think . . . I will."

In a few minutes, she reported, "He didn't stop. He's already around the bend."

"He'll be back. With reinforcements." Stuart was on his knees when Casey slid down to him. "We need to move farther inland."

"Not until I patch up that shoulder."

Blue Jay glanced at his chest, covered with blood. "Think you can handle it?"

"Why shouldn't I? I've had plenty of on-the-job training." As she stripped off his shirt, she added, "I didn't mean to help you kill that man back there. I didn't think . . . ." She kept her eyes on her work.

"Out here you don't think, Casey. You react, and you reacted quite well."

She looked up. "I still don't have to like it."

"Nobody likes it, but somebody has to do it."

"Now you sound like my father."

"The MIA Falcon told me about?"

"Yes." Casey fumbled in Stuart's pockets. "Where do you keep the damn bandages?"

Blue Jay pulled one of the plastic-sealed packs from a breast pocket and handed it to her. "I wondered why you and I weren't getting along."

"Now what are you talking about?" Casey ripped the packet apart and the strings fell out.

"Out here I remind you of your father."

"Well, out here, I don't have to be like him."

"Out here, what other choice do you have?"

CHAPTER
TWENTY-ONE

As Willie Tee labored under his end of the litter, he was thinking it wasn't possible for Lancaster to have become heavier, but the wounded man seemed to have done just that. Maybe it was the terrain. He and Pike were struggling through a narrow pass at the entrance of a long valley that would take them back into South Vietnam. They were getting closer and closer to home, even if they had to do it one foot at a time.

They had waited almost an hour for a chopper that had never come. No chopper meant Blue Jay had failed to find the patrol boat, or worse, he had found it and was dead. Maybe his body was being washed downstream at this very moment . . . toward Vietnam. Maybe it was like Pike said. Blue Jay had found the boat, but the woman had screwed it up for him. Who knew for sure? They might never know.

Was there something overhead? What was that sound?

Suddenly, the sky was raining Charlies, leaping from the side of the ravine, tumbling out of bushes, screaming like banshees. The litter fell to the ground as Eskew went to his knees. His rifle was ripped away and he was smothered with bodies. Eskew tried to throw them off, but each time, two more took their place.

"Pike! VC!"

Similar cries came from Pike and Falcon, then an arm across Eskew's throat cut off his wind. The man on top of him spoke English, somewhat.

"Stop! Kill general!"

Eskew stopped. Behind him, Pike did the same. Only Falcon still fought to get free, but two, then three Vietnamese held on tight and rode him to the ground.

Who were these guys? wondered Eskew. And how the hell did they know about Falcon? Weren't they too far south for that? Evidently not.

The Vietnamese rolled off and Eskew scrambled to his feet only to find himself staring at a row of rifles. The American froze. The men wore the dull green uniform of North Vietnamese regulars.

"On knees," ordered the Vietnamese. He gestured at his knees, then pointed at the ground.

Reluctantly, Pike and Eskew did as they were told, but Falcon had to be forced down.

Sweet Jesus! If he'd been more alert . . . instead of moping over what had happened to Blue Jay. Now the same thing was about to happen to them. Or maybe not—if they kept their wits about them. They still had their boot knives, and there was always the chance he and Pike could slip Falcon off into the jungle. Not much of a chance for Falcon, but what other chance did he have?

"Hand . . . ." The next word wouldn't come so the leader of the Charlies showed his prisoners how he wanted their hands behind their backs.

The Charlies tied the Americans' hands behind their backs, and that included Lancaster. When Eskew protested at the treatment of the unconscious man, he was slapped across his face.

"You! Shut up!"

Eskew looked the man in the eye. "Have your fun while you can, asshole. American troops are on the way."

The Vietnamese didn't follow.

"Americans. They come! Plenty choppers you see." Damn, thought Eskew, he was talking like some movie Indian. Why hadn't he taken time to learn the lingo from Blue Jay? Oh, Christ, how he'd love to see Blue Jay come riding in on a chopper.

A flashlight came out and the leader of the Vietnamese was in Eskew's face. "I watch. No choppers. No know you here." The leader of the Vietnamese pointed at the ground where they stood, then pointed to the north. "Americans . . . no know you . . . ."

"Downriver," finished Pike sourly.

The Charlie looked at Pike and nodded. "Americans no know you downriver."

Christ, thought Eskew, this Charlie knows more than we do.

The leader of the NVA stood up, and in the light from the flashlight, Eskew saw the man was affected by "the thousand-yard stare," a condition sometimes seen in soldiers who had experienced too much killing. This guy was going to be one tough nut to crack.

"Search them," Bien said in Vietnamese. "I will not have my throat cut like those fool Cambodians."

Hands flew over the Americans. Their boot knives were found, along with an assortment of field equipment. The equipment was split up among the NVA, making smiles bloom all around.

Eskew watched the Charlies as they traded the equipment. We're not finished yet, you bastards. If there are Americans on the southeastern trail that means Long Bien has crossed the border, probably in force. Your best option is to press deeper into Cambodia. Which gives us a chance. Like any other soldier you have to rest, and from the looks of you, you're as exhausted as we are. Maybe more so. If he and Pike sat back to back . . . .

Bien knelt in front of Falcon. "So this is the man who has worked so hard to avoid meeting me."

His men laughed.

Their leader whirled around, staring them into silence. The general had been destined to be captured. By him. Bien returned his attention to Falcon. "You. Me. TV." He threw his arms out. "The world see. Me. You."

Falcon looked away and allowed a little boredom to slip into his stare.

The Charlie eyed the Americans on their knees. "No chance. You have no chance." He stood up and snapped out orders.

Security was sent out, and canteens were opened

and drunk as if filled with champagne. The Vietnamese slapped each other on the back, congratulated each other, and made derisive remarks about the Americans' fighting ability. It was true. Once you took away their mighty weapons and aircraft, they could be beaten and beaten quite easily.

"I have him!" Bien reported to headquarters. "I have the general and I took him alive." Bien shook his head. "No, sir. Alive."

Bien listened for a few moments. "I understand. I am to rendezvous with the patrol boat two hundred meters south of their last ambush site . . . . Yes, sir, I have that location on my map." Bien signed off and said in his pidgin English, "Man killed at boat. Woman, too."

"Oh, my God!" groaned Falcon, and for a long while he stared at the ground in front of him.

✳   ✳   ✳

Sergeant Major Harmon came through the doors of the command bunker on the run and scanned the room for the OD or the XO. He saw both men behind the Plexiglas wall of the OD's office in the rear of the room. The two officers were waiting out the return of the search parties in the isolation of the officer of the day's office.

Good, thought Harmon. Lately, the OD had been getting on everyone's nerves as he watched his career go up in flames. But now more than one career might be in jeopardy, from Long Bien all the way to the White House.

Harmon opened the door without being acknowledged. The exec was trying to distract the OD with stories of better days when he'd been in command of a company of tanks and had dry land to run them on. The exec looked up as Harmon let himself in.

"Sir, we've got a problem."

"What is it this time?" asked the exec with a sigh.

"There's a reporter inside the compound."

The exec sat up. "What are you talking about? I thought you said the perimeter was secure."

"Yes, sir, and I personally made the rounds and told them to keep all civilians out."

"Then what happened?" asked Daniels from behind his desk.

"I don't know, sir."

"Well," said the exec, "throw the bum out. I've got a mission to perform and I don't want some reporter wandering around inside my perimeter."

"I've tried to, sir, but he won't leave. He's demanding to speak to whoever's in charge. He says he knows the CIC isn't here and that we're operating across the border."

"What?" asked both officers, glancing at each other.

"Who is this joker?" demanded the exec.

"Robert Sligh of the *Times*."

"My God!" said the exec, standing up and heading for the door. "That's all I need. Some pinko reporter demanding an accounting of my invasion of Cambodia. My illegal invasion of Cambodia."

"You had to do it, sir," said the officer of the day. "It was the only way to get Falcon back." Right about now Daniels would kiss anyone's ass. He had four years left until retirement and two kids to put through college.

"And we were obligated to assist the Vietnamese," replied the exec. "But people like Robert Sligh don't understand so he's certainly not going to understand my invading a neutral country to rescue my commanding officer."

The officer of the day followed them out the door and across the command center, where the exec stopped at the double doors. A newly assigned sergeant eyed the three men and fingered his sidearm.

"You stay here, Daniels," said the exec, "and keep an eye on things. I can take care of Mr. Sligh."

Daniels' shoulders sagged. No one had a clue as to where Falcon was and already there had been reports of six soldiers with broken arms or legs from the units operating across the border. This whole operation was being run in the dark, and Daniels wasn't just thinking about conditions on the jungle floor.

"And," added the XO, "get someone at the Pentagon to call his publisher. Publishers seem to have a better grasp of national security than most reporters."

The exec and the sergeant major went out the door and down the hall, where the exec was hailed by an officer leaning out the mess hall door. At the door was posted an MP.

"When the hell do we get out of here?"

Evidently not a career man, thought the XO. "When I'm damn good and ready."

The exec continued down the hall and up the stairs to the ground floor. An MP opened the door for him and the exec stepped outside. Emerging from the air-conditioning into the tropical night was like hitting a wet sheet left over the door.

"Where is this joker?"

"Over here," Sligh said. "And I'm not joking."

The reporter sat in a jeep, feet propped up on the narrow dash. He smoked a cigar and blew smoke rings over the glass. The MPs flanking the jeep looked from the exec to Sligh and back at the exec again.

"Handcuff that man! He's not to run loose inside this facility."

Sligh's feet came off the dash as he tossed the cigar away. "You can't do that. I'll have your ass in court. I'm an accredited journalist."

The MPs looked at the exec.

"The judge won't be asking about your accreditation, Mr. Sligh, but how you came to be trespassing inside a military installation."

Sligh clambered down from the jeep. When he did, the MPs' pistols came out. They followed the reporter over to where the exec stood.

"Throwing me in jail won't stop the world from learning about your illegal invasion of Cambodia."

The general looked around. Besides the MPs how many others had heard the accusation? For sure the guards at the bunker door, maybe other soldiers drifting toward the confrontation.

Everything about the incursion—that's what they'd decided to call the operation—was to stay inside the command bunker. Inside the command bunker they operated on secured frequencies, telling anyone who asked that Falcon's chopper had actually gone down on this side of the border.

Most had accepted the explanation, not wanting to think otherwise. Even the search parties, with the exception of their leaders, thought that their search for Falcon was being conducted on the Vietnamese side of the border. And the crews who'd been with Falcon's chopper when it had gone down—the other Huey and the two Cobra gunships—were in quarantine. At this very moment, they were being warned what would happen to their careers—military or civilian—if they gained a reputation as soldiers who couldn't keep a secret, especially one dealing with national security.

The executive officer gestured at the base camp. "Do you really have a story, Mr. Sligh? For an invasion of that magnitude I would think more would be going on. It looks pretty quiet, except for the drill I'm conducting."

"This is no drill."

"And you're in serious trouble this time. This isn't helping some Buddhist monk set himself on fire."

Sligh got in the exec's face. "I resent that!" The MPs grabbed the reporter, restraining him. "I had nothing to do with the immolations. Can't you give these people credit for thinking for themselves? Or do you see a commie under every bed?"

"I see one in front of me. You're in cahoots with the enemy, and not for the first time. I'll take my chances with what you report, as I have in the past. I don't think the people of the United States are going to take the word of a traitor."

"I'm the traitor? I'm the one in the wrong? Look at

what you're doing to this country."

"We're trying to save it from your communist friends."

"And in the process, destroying it!"

"Mr. Sligh, I'm not about to stand here and debate the merits of this war with you. You haven't once covered our successes with the Pacification Program."

"Because there haven't been any."

The exec's face turned purple with rage. "Seize this man. Throw him in the stockade! I may have to tolerate such garbage outside my perimeter but not inside."

Over the MPs' "yes, sirs," Sligh shouted, "I demand to speak to the CIC! I demand you produce him. I will not talk with some second-rater."

"You can talk to him at the conclusion of this drill."

As the MPs dragged Sligh back to the jeep, he taunted, "You can't produce him, can you? He's not here, is he? He's in Cambodia, isn't he?"

"That, Mr. Sligh, is no longer any concern of yours." To Harmon, the exec said, "Have the MPs police up everyone within the sound of that man's voice."

The sergeant major hurried over to the door of the command bunker and whispered his orders. The MPs fanned out, rounding up soldiers.

Sligh was shoved into the jeep, where he grabbed the windshield and pulled himself to his feet. "You can torture me, you can kill me, but you can't kill this story! Casey Blackburn also has this story."

A chill ran through the exec. How'd this reporter know Casey Blackburn was with Falcon? Where was the leak? And how had Sligh slipped inside the perimeter. "Don't be so paranoid, Mr. Sligh. You'll be well taken care of . . . even when you're brought up on charges."

Sligh opened his mouth to shout something else, but one of the MPs raised his nightstick. Sligh shut up and sat down. And he sat down as much from the threat of the nightstick as the fact that he would come out of this not only with the invasion story, but also with a story about a tunnel leading into the American compound. Yes, life was coming up roses, even if roses didn't come in black.

As Sergeant Harmon and the exec watched the jeep move away, they both shared the same thought. Casey Blackburn hated this war as much as anyone. She'd never gotten over her father's disappearance and probable death, and it was Blackburn who was out there with the CIC. If Blackburn came out of this alive, anything that woman wrote would start knocking over careers like so many dominoes.

"Master Sergeant?"

"Yes, sir?"

"For what it's worth, have those MPs brought to the command bunker and quarantined with the other men."

"Yes, sir. For what it's worth, sir."

The exec stared at Harmon before reentering the bunker. He had never seen a war as toxic as Vietnam had been to officers and enlisted men alike. Its poison spread everywhere.

CHAPTER TWENTY-TWO

The North Vietnamese were headed for the river when Casey and Stuart ran into them. Both parties were using the same trail, but the Vietnamese were relaxed and noisy while the unarmed Americans were tense and watchful. Stuart heard the approaching soldiers and hustled Casey off the trail.

Moments later, the point man strolled by, only a few feet in front of the rest of the column. This puzzled Stuart. These were NVA regulars who were horsing around and breaking the rules of night security. Then he saw the members of his team with their hands tied behind their backs and Lancaster on a stretcher. The sergeant did not moan nor did he move.

"Good God!" said Casey, barely remembering to whisper. "They've got Falcon! What are we going to do?"

Stuart watched the party disappear down the trail. "Take him away from them again."

"But you're wounded and we don't have any weapons."

"You came up with the last idea. Got any more?"

"You wouldn't want to hear it. My last one almost got you killed."

But Stuart had started off, trailing the Vietnamese and their prisoners. "They'll stop at the river."

Casey followed him. "Unless that patrol boat returns."

Blue Jay turned his upper body around and looked over his shoulder. The pain in his chest and shoulder made him grimace. "Thanks, Casey. I really needed to hear that."

Because the Vietnamese weren't as alert as they normally would be, Casey and Stuart were able to stay within thirty to forty feet of the column. At the river, the Charlies stopped, put out a semicircle of security against the riverbank, and did more relaxing. Because he was wearing the black pj's and spoke the language, Blue Jay slipped inside their perimeter and brought back the camp's layout. Casey had been ordered to wait a hundred yards or so down the trail. As she did, she realized the jungle darkness no longer frightened her as it once had, proving you could get used to just about anything.

"I count fifteen or sixteen Charlies. One-third posted as sentries, another third with the prisoners, and the rest along the river. Their command post is in the middle of the perimeter, and that's where the radio is. The prisoners are twenty to thirty feet from the radio."

"Then they are meeting the boat."

"My guess is our people have put so many troops on this side of the border the only way Charlie feels safe is by moving Falcon deeper into Cambodia, and the quickest way is by boat."

"Wait a minute," said Casey, coming off the log she had been sitting on. "Are you saying the United States has invaded Cambodia?"

"Long Bien would storm Hanoi to get Falcon back."

Casey stamped her foot. "Dammit! And I'm not there to cover it."

"Nobody's covering it. There's no way the press knows about this."

She considered that. "Unless Charlie's told some reporter."

"What do you mean?"

"Oh, nothing. I just know someone who has contacts on both sides of the war."

"Then don't ever let me meet him."

"I don't like him myself, but he sure knows his way around this war."

"That shouldn't present any problem, if you don't care who your sources are."

Casey didn't think this the time or the place to mention her interview with Ho Chi Minh, the coup that had landed her in-country. Instead, she asked, "What are we going to do?"

"I've got to get to that radio." Stuart glanced down the trail. "With a radio I can drop an airborne company on their location in less than five minutes, artillery even sooner. A location's all Long Bien's waiting for."

"But you could get killed—Falcon, too."

"At this point I'm willing to take that chance. Falcon would probably go along with it, too."

"How long do you need to get your message off?"

"Only seconds. Just time to change frequencies and broadcast Falcon's location. Leave the mike keyed and they can zero in on our location."

"But to get to the radio . . . ."

"Has to be done quietly. So it doesn't matter that I don't have a rifle or pistol. What I really need is the knife I dropped on the patrol boat."

"Maybe one of the sentries . . . ."

"NVA aren't famous for carrying much equipment. Their basic issue is a rifle and ammo, a canteen, a small bag of rice, and another uniform." Blue Jay stared at the stand of bamboo. "I've still got my Swiss Army knife. If I cut down one of those stalks and put a point on it—"

"Use it like a bayonet!"

He smiled at her. "Nothing like being stuck in the jungle with an army brat."

"I'm not an army brat!"

"You sure sound like one."

They went to work on the bamboo, and when they were finished, Stuart said, "The Chinese made the first bombs out of bamboo." He ran his fingers up the shaft to its point. "The inside of the tube is so slick . . . if I had something to propel a sharpened sliver along like a crossbow . . . bamboo shafts go in deep and they go in fast. That's why Charlie uses them in his *punji* pits. Go right through the sole of any boot."

"Would the elastic in my bra work?"

Stuart stared at her. "Now why didn't I think of that?"

"I can think of two very good reasons."

Stuart smiled, then selected another stalk and worked on it while Casey held the shaft down. When he had the shaft as he wanted it, he took it over to the log where, with his knife and the assistance of Casey's hands, he fashioned slivers of bamboo about half a foot long and half an inch wide. A second piece of bamboo was split in half and fashioned into a mini-cross-bow.

"How will you fire it?"

Blue Jay pointed at his left arm. "With my hand."

"The one you were shot in?"

He nodded. "I won't have to move the arm, just the fingers. And I'm going to have you tie my arm up higher, across my chest so I can reach the bamboo shaft."

"You've lost me. How are you going to hold up the barrel?"

"I won't have to. I'm going to have you strap it on my good arm. Then all I'll have to do is point and shoot. I'm a fairly good snap shooter."

"Snap shooter?"

"Just point and fire. I don't do as well if I take aim."

"My father was like that. Just point and fire."

"You probably could, too."

Casey shook her head. "No, no. I don't want to kill any more."

"And I hope you don't have to." He gestured at the slivers. "Instead of firing bullets, I'll fire these."

"But you'll only have one shot. That's a lot riding on one shot."

"I'm making two. You can strap one over and one

247

under my arm. If two shots won't get the job done, accuracy won't be my problem, timing will." He smiled. "Time for your bra, Miss Blackburn."

Casey flushed, then turned away and hustled off into the darkness. After glancing around to see that no one was there—wasn't that nuts!—she reached under her fatigue blouse, up behind her, unhooking the bra. She pulled one arm, and then the other, through the sleeves and out of the straps. The night air slipped under her blouse and cooled her breasts.

Casey glanced around again—she couldn't help herself—then stuffed the bra in her pocket. Her shirttail back in, she returned to the log where she and Stuart fashioned the weapon he had described. They used string from Stuart's bottomless pockets to tie both shafts to his right arm. Finished, Casey stood back and watched as Stuart swung the arm around. Maybe the damn thing would work after all. Maybe.

"I'm going in with you," she said.

"No. You come down the trail after the area has been secured. By then, there'll be a chopper waiting to return you to Long Bien."

Casey shook her head. "I helped you get on that boat and I can help you now."

"This is different, Casey."

"How?"

"This time I may not be coming back."

"An even better reason to tag along."

"You don't back off, do you?"

"I wouldn't have this job if I did."

"And see where that got you."

"Don't try to change the subject."

"Casey, those are hardened NVA regulars. Everything you've been through up until now has been nothing compared to tangling with those guys."

Casey remembered the helicopter crash, her mad dash through the jungle, the bandits wanting to rape her, and almost being killed on the patrol boat. Nothing could be worse than that. On top of it all, it was raining again. Funny, she'd never noticed. "I'm still going with you."

"You might have to kill again."

"I'll take my chances."

"I'm in no shape to stop you. Hell, I can't even order you not to go. You don't seem to have the proper respect for the chain of command. What you should consider is that those boys along the river are celebrating right now, but the moment we're detected, they'll be all over us."

"Sorry," said Casey, shaking her head, "but when I remember what Lancaster did, coming down through the canopy, running point and taking bullets for me, I can't let you go in alone."

"Sure you're not looking for an exciting end to this story you're going to write?"

Casey glanced at the ground. "I don't think there's a story here at all. Men doing their jobs? What's so special about that?"

Stuart stared at her, then he took her by the hand and led her down the trail toward the NVA encampment.

CHAPTER
TWENTY-THREE

Blue Jay parted the bushes between him and the center of the North Vietnamese camp. The soldiers were still celebrating, euphoria flowing like wine. The guards posted around the Americans taunted their prisoners. The captured members of the Blue Jay team were bunched up, their backs to each other as if frightened of the Charlies.

Blue Jay nodded. With their backs together, he could count on Pike and Eskew having their hands free when all hell broke loose, and sooner or later, all hell would break loose.

A single Charlie sat in the middle of the camp, next to the radio. Blue Jay would bet that man was leader of this unruly pack. Any RTO would've joined in the celebration, but not the leader. Not someone who'd engineered the recapture of Falcon. That man would hold himself aloof, waiting for proper congratulations, and those congratulations could only come from his superiors.

STEVE BROWN

For the leader to be manning the radio was a stroke of luck. Not only would they gain access to the radio by putting him out of action, but his soldiers would lose precious seconds reorganizing themselves after the loss of their leader. Blue Jay felt the pain radiating out from his shoulder, racing in long narrow fingers across his chest and down his side. Yes, and a bit of luck at this juncture of the contest would be greatly appreciated.

A hand touched his good shoulder.

"Now?" asked Casey.

The woman had pulled her hair up under a cap and soiled her face with dirt. She wore the uniform of a now-unconscious NVA sentry. Slung across her back was the sentry's rifle. Blue Jay had the woman wear the rifle over her back so she couldn't easily get at the weapon. With a weapon handy, Casey might be tempted to shoot someone, regardless of what she'd said about not wanting to kill again.

They didn't need any noise. So, the woman held the bamboo shaft with its sharpened point. He'd coached her on how to make the thrusting motion that could skewer a man, and over and over again reminded her to step forward and throw her weight into the lunge. But it would take more than a few practice stabs to turn this woman into an effective fighting machine, no matter how much promise she showed.

"Now," he said.

Casey gripped the shaft, surprised to learn she wasn't as frightened as she'd been in previous encounters with Charlie, and that made her even more afraid, afraid of what she was becoming.

251

As they approached the man and his radio, the leader of the Charlies stood up and turned his back on them. He shouted at those along the riverbank and the soldiers quieted down. When he turned around, Blue Jay almost took a shot at him, but before he could, the Charlie squatted down and picked up his canteen. Blue Jay lowered his arm and waited for the man to stand up so he could have a clear shot at his chest.

Bien became aware of the two figures, only meters away. He dropped the canteen and stood up. Off to his left, and coming up fast, was the sergeant of the guard. As well he should. Why were these two men away from their posts? With them missing there would be a hole in the perimeter big enough to drive a truck through. His men were out of control. The success of their mission had gone to their heads.

Bien pointed at Casey and Blue Jay. "Return these men to their posts, Sergeant."

The sergeant stared at Casey and Blue Jay. "I do not think they are part of our unit, sir."

"What?"

Bien looked at the figures again. Who did they belong to? One of them was Viet Cong. He could tell by the black clothing. Cursed Viet Cong! You never knew when or where they would turn up! The Viet Cong was pointing something at him. What did the fool want?

"Well, speak up." Something hit Bien in the throat.

What! *What?* Bien reached for his throat and found a stick protruding from it. What was this?

Another hit his chest, over the heart. What was happening here? These men were trying to kill him! As the taller one came closer, Bien saw his face and build.

Americans! They were Americans and they had come for the general. No! They could not have him!

Bien opened his mouth to warn his men, but he could do little more than gurgle. Something was wrong with his throat. He pulled out his pistol, but the American took the pistol from his hand and shoved him to the ground.

Bien fell hard, but now both hands were free to pull the stick out of his chest. He'd have to hurry. It seemed to be getting dark in this jungle. Darker than he had ever seen before.

The sergeant of the guard stepped toward the two strangers. What was going on here? Why had this soldier shoved the lieutenant to the ground. And now what was he doing with the radio?

Casey met the sergeant, not with the bamboo shaft but the stock of the sentry's rifle. She'd reversed the weapon and now held the rifle by its barrel. She clubbed the Vietnamese and the sergeant went to his knees. When he tried to get up, Casey tapped him again.

The man crumpled to the ground and Casey let out a sigh of relief. At least she hadn't had to kill. But she would've with that sharply pointed stick. Behind her, Blue Jay was talking in hushed tones, repeating the same numbers over and over again, followed by the phrase "No code, no code."

Casey knelt beside the sergeant and felt the man's neck. No pulse. Casey checked his chest. The man wasn't breathing. He was dead. Casey sat back, rifle falling across her lap. She'd killed again, even when she hadn't meant to.

FALLEN STARS

From the river came a shout. Casey scrambled to her feet and whirled around, bringing up the rifle and slipping off the safety. The patrol boat was returning, using a searchlight to locate their position. The Vietnamese along the river picked up their weapons and waved them over their heads. Several fired shots to identify their location. One of the soldiers ran up the embankment toward Blue Jay. Casey didn't understand a word the man was saying, but she saw Blue Jay drop the handset and fumble around for a weapon.

When the soldier was less than ten feet away, Casey opened up with the rifle, and open up she did, her nervous fumbling having switched the rifle from single fire to automatic. The AK-47 spewed bullets, its arc rising with the barrel. Most of the bullets flew over the head of the Charlie, but two hit the man, first in the groin, then the chest. The soldier was thrown backwards and Casey was left to stare at the rifle as it jumped around in her hands, finally leaping to the ground. Her hands shook; her body trembled. The rifle lay at her feet. At least it had finally stopped firing.

Blue Jay grabbed her from where he lay on the ground. "Get down, Casey!"

She did, and all hell broke loose.

The Vietnamese guarding the American prisoners looked in the direction of the command post. Why was someone firing inside the perimeter? And you didn't mark your position by firing your weapon on automatic. Bien would have the man's head.

As the four guards stared toward the interior of the perimeter, they were knocked flat by Pike, Eskew, and

254

Falcon. Pike and Eskew wrenched rifles away and shot their guards while the Vietnamese lay on the ground. That left two guards to scramble to their feet and turn their weapons on the Americans, specifically Falcon. The guards had their orders. If anything went wrong, this American wasn't to leave Cambodia alive.

Pike threw himself across Falcon and let go with another burst from the rifle he had seized from one of the guards. Pike's bullets caught the guard across the chest as the Vietnamese's bullets hit him in the same place. Willie Tee killed the last guard, then pulled Pike off Falcon and cradled the dying man in his arms.

Pike smiled up at him. "It's okay, Willie Tee. I was getting sick and tired of all this killing." He closed his eyes and was gone.

"Willie Tee! Pike!" shouted Blue Jay. "Take the river!"

Falcon was on his feet, but Eskew grabbed him and sent the general in a running stumble into the bushes. "Stay in there, sir!"

"Untie me!"

"No time! Got a boat to meet." And the black man charged the river with a wild scream.

The soldiers along the riverbank were confused. First, there had been the firing inside their own perimeter—they had dropped below the riverbank as bullets had zinged in their direction—and now they were being attacked by some wild man. Where had he come from?

When one of the Charlies stuck his head up for a look-see, Eskew blew the man's head off. He kicked another man in the face and leaped off the riverbank, stumbling into the water. One of the Charlies tried to shoot Eskew as he went by, but when Eskew hit the water, he rolled to one side, firing backwards toward the riverbank. His bullets hit all around the remaining Charlies. One went down and played possum. The other followed Eskew into the water.

Eskew got to his feet to find a rifle in his face. He jerked his head to one side as the rifle exploded. Bright lights blinded him, and the ear on that side went deaf. Still, Eskew could make out forms in the light from the patrol boat. He stuck his rifle in the man's stomach and split the Charlie in half.

When Eskew looked up, he saw another Charlie charging off the embankment. The man was on him before he could get away. But this one had forgotten about that first long step off the bank, and as he came down, his rifle jerked down, sending its burst into Eskew's legs and knocking them out from under him.

Eskew fell back, half in, half out of the water. The Charlie's hard charge propelled the Vietnamese into the shallows. When the Vietnamese turned around to come ashore, Eskew killed him with the last of his bullets. The soldier threw up his rifle and fell back, in front of the approaching gunboat.

A frightened Charlie, the one who'd played possum while Eskew had run amuck, regained his composure when he saw the American lying on his back at the water's edge. Before Willie Tee could locate another weapon, the Charlie was standing over him and grinning . . . up to the moment his head exploded.

Blue Jay had found Lt. Bien's handgun. Stuart's next victim was a sentry moving toward the center of the perimeter, then another charging their position.

Casey looked up to see Blue Jay straddling the radio and scanning the area for more Vietnamese. For the moment, the Blue Jay Team was in charge of the shoreline, but how long could that last? They were trapped between the collapsing sentries and the arriving patrol boat.

The light on the boat searched the riverbank. On the bow, a sailor locked and loaded the .50-caliber. Casey crawled over and picked up the dead sergeant's rifle. But what good would a rifle be against a machine gun that could take off an arm or leg with a single round? And if the sailors on the patrol boat didn't like the odds, they could simply lay offshore and hose down the riverbank, then come ashore and pick up the pieces. Sweet Jesus, how the hell did she know how everything would play out?

In the air overhead, a small explosion lit up the night. Casey glanced up as a flare sizzled and popped above her. Blue Jay found a Charlie staring at the flare. It was the last thing the man saw as he pitched backwards and died watching the descending light. Blue Jay stuffed the pistol in his belt and picked up the radio handset.

In a remarkably quiet voice, he said, "Drop fifty. Fire for effect. And take out the patrol boat. It has a .50 caliber on board."

The remaining sentries weren't cowed by the flare but took their cue from it. It didn't matter who you killed. Just charge the center, killing everyone there. One of the dead would have to be the general.

Blue Jay jerked the pistol out again and pulled Casey down beside him. "Now it'll really hit the fan."

"Where's our support? You promised me reinforcements."

"In a minute."

"In a minute we could all be dead!"

"Yeah, but what a way to go!"

As the remaining sentries rushed their position, air force Phantoms soared out of the night under light from a second artillery flare. The Phantoms were visible for only a couple of seconds as they shook the air, diving for the patrol boat. The sailors swung their machine gun up and around, but the Phantoms were gone before the barrel could be trained on either plane. The first bomb exploded on the port side, spraying the craft with water and knocking a sailor over the side. The second bomb blew the boat out of the river.

The explosions staggered those on shore, forcing them to their knees. One man was even flattened. Another flare ignited overhead as the Charlies staggered to their feet and prepared a final charge. Nothing had changed. Kill anything that moved. That had been Lt. Bien's final order.

Blue Jay was on the radio again. "Direct hit on the boat . . . . Yes. Please bring in reinforcements. Our position's about to be overrun." He gave the handset to Casey. "Reinforcements on the way." He picked up the pistol again and threw a shot at an advancing Charlie. "Still with us, Falcon?"

"Yo!" came the cry from across the battlefield.

A sentry took a cautious shot at Blue Jay, and Stuart

returned fire. Bullets zinged over Casey's head as she flattened herself to the ground.

"They're about to wet their pants back in Long Bien," said Blue Jay from beside her. "Tell them Falcon's okay. Push to talk, and don't forget to release the button when you want to listen."

Casey stared at the handset. She knew how to do that. Someone had taught her how earlier in the day—from the enemy base camp, only a few hours ago. A few hours ago! It seemed like an eternity.

The Phantoms were angry, invisible hornets streaking overhead, looking for another target. When they roared off, Casey heard the choppers. She looked up and saw soldiers standing on the skids of Hueys and taking potshots at the remaining sentries. The Charlies finally broke and ran, disappearing into the jungle.

Someone squawked on the handset. Casey pushed down the push-to-talk button and the man stopped squawking. "Long Bien, are you there?" When no one answered she repeated herself, then remembered to take her finger off the push-to-talk button.

"—is Long Bien. Who the hell is this?"

"Casey Blackburn."

"Who?"

"Casey Blackburn. A reporter."

"Aw, shit!" came back the reply.

Casey was telling the voice on the radio that Falcon was okay when her grip loosened on the handset and the instrument fell from her hand. Across the battlefield and under the light from another flare, the leader of the Cambodian bandits had one arm around Falcon's neck and his pistol at the general's head. Behind him stood four of his fellow bandits, rifles at the ready. The bandit's English was enough to make Casey begin trembling all over again.

"The woman! Or I kill this man!"

Falcon struggled to free himself, but the bandit only tightened his grip around the general's throat. Barely able to see over the American's shoulder, no one could get a shot at the bandit.

American soldiers leaped from the Hueys and dropped to one knee, covering the bandits and Falcon. The captain of the unit looked from the man in the black pajamas with an arm strapped across his chest to the blonde in the uniform of a North Vietnamese regular. Casey's pith helmet had fallen off in all the excitement.

"Just who the hell's in charge down here?"

"Looks like I am," said Casey, pushing herself to her knees.

The captain gave her a funny look and Blue Jay stopped maneuvering for a head shot. He stared at her. Casey stared, too, but at the pistol pointed at Falcon's head. She really didn't want to be swapped for Falcon, but she didn't see any other way.

"You're not to come over here, Casey," said Falcon.

Maybe she shouldn't. Probably she couldn't. Her legs were like rubber, her stomach hollow. In the light from the flares, she could see the leader of the Charlies lying at her feet with his hands on the bamboo sliver in his heart. Would this never end? Someone had to make this end.

The bandit leader called for her again.

"Help me up," she asked the American captain.

"Stay where you are, Casey," said Blue Jay. "You don't have to go over there. I can take him from here."

She forced a smile as she was pulled to her feet. "You never were much good with a fixed target. You said so yourself."

Stuart put his good arm around her. "Casey, I've come too far to lose you now."

She smiled at Stuart, then glanced at Falcon being held by the bandit. "I'll see what I can work out."

She shook loose from his arm and forced herself to walk over to where Falcon and the bandits stood, a walk that felt longer than the forced-march through Cambodia.

When Falcon refused to leave, the bandit stuck his pistol in the general's face and pulled back the hammer.

"I'm not leaving you, Casey," Falcon said.

"You have to, sir. You have an obligation to our country."

"But it's not right."

Casey smiled at the tall, lean warrior. "Just don't give up on me like my father did."

"You go!" said the bandit, his arm around Casey, his other hand holding the pistol to her head.

Falcon shook his head, then moved toward the helicopter, careful to stay out of the Americans' line of fire. Everyone was staring at Casey: the young Americans with their rifles at the ready and Stuart with his pistol at his side, ready to snap off a shot if given the opportunity. Overhead another flare popped and lit up the night.

When the bandit turned around to tell his men they were moving out, Casey brought up a hand and rammed a bamboo sliver into the side of the man's throat. The bandit jerked back. His free hand fell away from Casey, and he pulled at the stick with the hand that held the pistol. His eyes widened as he saw the blood on the stick, now running hot down the side of his throat. The woman had killed him. Well, there was an answer for that. He brought up the pistol.

"No!" shouted Casey, slapping the pistol away.

Her hands hit the flat side of the weapon. The pistol slammed into the bandit's chest and discharged. Casey screamed as the gun went off. She closed her eyes, only opening them when the man's hand slipped off, sliding across her uniform blouse. The bandit leader finally let go and fell to the ground. The bullet had gone in under his chin, exiting through the top of his skull.

Casey shuddered as brains oozed out of the man's head and the bandit collapsed on the ground. His men stared, open-mouthed, at their leader. As they did, the line of Americans opened fire. Casey flinched at the sudden explosion, then again when the bandits crumpled to the ground, weapons falling from their hands.

Now the battlefield was quiet, the only sound the *swish-swish-swish* of helicopter blades and the sizzle of a flare as it drifted to earth. The flare illuminated the man lying at her feet. Another man she'd killed. A man she'd wanted to kill. Planned to kill. Had to kill. None of that made her feel any better.

Blue Jay was there, holding her with his good arm. "Perfect, Casey, just perfect."

Casey glanced at the man missing the top of his skull, his fellow bandits dead from the Americans' fire, and the wounded Eskew and Lancaster and the dead Pike being hustled onto the waiting chopper.

"No, Blue Jay, I don't think so. I don't think any of this turned out right, much less perfect."

ABOUT THE AUTHOR

After graduating from the University of North Alabama with a degree in history and political science, Steve Brown served as a combat platoon leader with the 25th Infantry Division in South Vietnam. He lives with his family in South Carolina. You can contact Steve through www.chicksprings.com.

Of Love and War is a tale of intrigue and suspense,
revealing startling information "classified" until now.
Like Gone with the Wind, The Winds of War,
and Doctor Zhivago, it is also a powerful love story
set against the backdrop of one of the most tragic
and exciting moments in history.

Available at your local bookstore.
ISBN 0-9670273-0-6

Lifeguard and runaway finder Susan Chase goes looking
for a missing girl and finds herself in over her head–in
murder. A fast-paced, hard-boiled tale with a Gen-X
twist. Rated R for language, violence, and *attitude!*

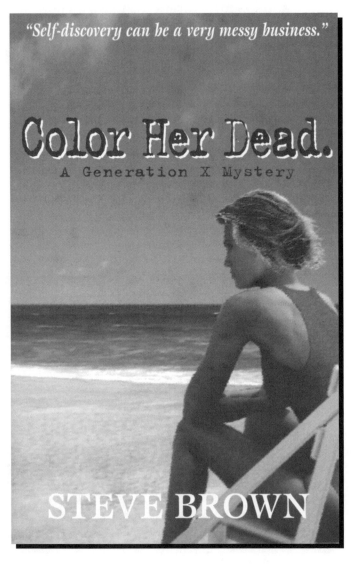

"*Self-discovery can be a very messy business.*"

Color Her Dead.
A Generation X Mystery

STEVE BROWN

Available at your local bookstore.
ISBN 0-9670273-1-4

A free man after 22 years and 22 days in prison,
Raymond Lister has set out on a mission of revenge
against the woman who put him behind bars. For rape.
Jean Fox, nationally syndicated radio psychologist, is preparing
for her only daughter's wedding. Jean has everything under
control—except her most terrible secret.

From the author of *Color Her Dead* and *Black Fire*

STEVE
BROWN

radio
secrets